Cowboy Confessions

by

Gail MacMillan

Cowboy Confessions

Cover Art by *Debbie Taylor*

The Wild Rose Press, Inc.
PO Box 708
Adams Basin, NY 14410-0708
Visit us at www.thewildrosepress.com

Publishing History
First Yellow Rose Edition, 2016
Print ISBN 978-1-5092-0939-2
Digital ISBN 978-1-5092-0940-8

Published in the United States of America

"What?" Astounded by the offer, Jessi stared up at him.

"Dance. With you to support me, I think I might be able to handle this old tune."

"Ross, what are you up to?" She narrowed her eyes as she looked up at him.

"Nothing, nothing. The desire to try just came to me. But if you don't want to…"

"No, no, of course not." She stood. *Can't discourage any bit of initiative he's willing to try.*

He laid his cane up against the veranda railing and took her into his arms. For a moment, he hesitated, looking up at her through the soft black veil of summer night shadows. A butterfly feeling fluttered inside her.

"It's been a long time." he muttered, and Jessi didn't know if he meant since he'd danced or since he'd held a woman in his arms.

"All the more reason to get back in the game." She struggled to sound casual.

"Okay, let's give this a go."

As he drew her against his body and his hand found the small of her back, she caught the scent of his after shave and was struck by a myriad of sensations so powerful they knocked her physically and emotionally off balance. When he started to move slowly, cautiously in time to the music, she stumbled.

"Sorry," he said softly, his lips close to her ear. "I warned you."

"My fault," she managed, but the words sounded falsetto and shaky. She tried for a recovery. "You're doing just fine."

"Am I?" He drew her out from him enough to look down into her face. "Am I, Jessi Wallace?"

Praise for Gail MacMillan

Heather, of *HEATHER FOR A HIGHLANDER*, was chosen as Best Heroine by the Trans Canada Romance Writers Maple Leaf Awards. Dr. William MacTavish placed as second favorite hero. The book's ending also received Honorable Mention.

"I love, love, loved this book [*HEATHER FOR A HIGHLANDER*]! It…begins in England with a murder, and ends with a fiery romance in British North America. And it's all because of a horse bet between brothers. I mean, isn't that how all good stories begin?"

~*Romance Novels for the Beach*

"Read in one sitting, which hardly ever happens for me. Truly engaging. I would definitely pick up another book by this author."

~*a judge at TransCRW competition*

"Be prepared to be hooked on the first word of the first page and go on to the next with anticipation."

~*Rebecca Melvin, Publisher, Double Edge Press*

"Gail MacMillan's stories delight the senses and brighten the dark days of winter like a candle glowing on a windowsill."

~*Sue Owens Wright, author, newspaper columnist*

"I love this little adventure [*HOLDING OFF FOR A HERO*]!…surprises…one light, wonderful read."

~*The Romance Reviews (4 Stars)*

"Not sure who I like better, [the] German Shepherd, the Pug, or the sexy next door neighbor."

~*Matilda, Coffee Time Romance & More (5 Cups)*

"Not your typical romance story [*SHADOWS OF LOVE*], but I couldn't put it down."

~*Michelle, Cocktails and Books (4 Cups)*

Dedication

To my equine advisers Joan, Jessi, and Shirley,
who do their best to keep me "horse wise"

~*~

Other Books by Gail MacMillan
available from The Wild Rose Press, Inc.

Non-Fiction:
How My Heart Finds Christmas
To All the Dogs I've Loved Before

Historical Romance:
Privateer's Princess
Highland Harry
Heather for a Highlander
Shadows of Love
Caledonian Privateer
Lady and the Beast

Contemporary Romance:
Phantom and the Fugitive
Cowboy and the Crusader
Counterfeit Cowboy
Rogue's Revenge
Holding Off for a Hero
Ghost of Winters Past

Chapter One

"Now the final event of the day, the big ticket item of rodeo, bull riding. And here's the man you've all been waiting to see, World Champion Bull Rider two years in a row, the rock star of rodeo, Ross Turner!"

As the announcer's voice blared out across the rain-soaked arena, Jessi Wallace stood behind the high rails of the fence on the far side, her fingers tightening on the top bar. Bull riding had to be the most dangerous sport in rodeoing. No matter how often she witnessed it, she caught herself holding her breath each time a cowboy burst out in front of a crowd on one of those huge bucking, twisting animals.

Today, as she squinted through the June mizzle, she was more tense than usual. Ross Turner was the son of Bob and Laura Turner, good friends of her parents. The Turner ranch was only fifty miles from her parents' place. She'd known Ross for years, even competing against him a few times in local gymkhanas before he'd joined the rodeo circuit and turned pro. Over the past decade they'd drifted apart, jobs and differing interests the major reasons, but now concern for him rushed over her. With rain turning the arena slick with mud, he'd be facing a treacherous added challenge.

Please, please let him be okay.

Bull and man burst out into the arena. Jessi's breath hiccupped. The animal bucked and whirled in an attempt to dislodge the man hanging on to his back by the strength of a single hand and arm. So far a good ride. It looked like Ross would make it to the horn and be once again on his way to another World Championship.

Then it happened. The Brahma lost its footing, skidded, and upset. It landed on its back. Ross Turner was pinned under a ton of bovine flesh.

Oh, dear God!

Bull fighters raced to distract the animal as it struggled to its hooves, dragging with it the man, his hand tangled in the rope he'd used to stay aboard.

Jessi closed her eyes. She couldn't bear to watch.

When she looked again, the Brahma was being herded into the alley that led back to the paddocks while paramedics rushed to the man lying immobile in the mud and rain. The palomino mare beside her nudged her shoulder, and she drew the animal's head against her for comfort.

Thank God Mom and Dad aren't in the audience.

Knowing how her parents felt about the Turner family, it would have been almost as if their own child had been crushed under that massive animal.

Ross. I have to find out how he is. The first aid station—that's where they'll take him.

Leading the mare with strides so long and swift the animal had to break into a trot to keep pace, she headed for the trailer that served as a medical center on the rodeo grounds.

"Come on, Maisy," she urged the shy, apprehensive horse. "This is no time to act up."

"Hey, Horse Whisperer!" Ginny Morgan's sarcastic shout stopped her. She turned to look at the young woman in designer jeans, leather jacket, and black Stetson striding toward her on hand-tooled boots. In her right hand she held a quirt. "What's the story on my mare? Did you get the kinks out of her? Will she be ready to race tomorrow?"

"Ginny, I don't have time to talk to you now. A friend has been injured."

"So what?" the woman blocked her path. "You're not a paramedic. You can't help. Now tell me, what's the story on my horse?"

God, I don't need this now, but I'll have to deal with it. Otherwise I'll never get to find out about Ross.

"Maisy isn't cut out to be a barrel-racing horse." Jessi faced the scowl distorting the other woman's otherwise beautiful face. "My two weeks of working with her has only proven the fact. She hasn't the speed or agility. In fact, it will take a lot more work to give her the confidence she'll need to be a show horse of any kind."

"Are you telling me you drove all the way down here to return her to me no better than she was?" Anger snapped in the words as rain dripped off the brim of her hat. "When you asked me to meet you, I assumed I was going to discover stellar results. You're touted as the best in the business." She grabbed the reins from Jessi. "Let me have a go at this lazy little witch. Maybe a few good swift cracks will make her move." She raised the quirt she carried.

The mare jerked back and half-reared, eyes showing white. Passersby jumped away from the cavorting animal.

"That won't work!" Jessi tried to recover the reins. "It will only make her more apprehensive."

3

"Apprehensive! Damn it, if that's the case, she's only good for dog food. I'll sell her off tomorrow."

"I'll buy her!" The words were out of Jessi's mouth before she gave them thought.

"Buy her? For what? You've already said she's no good for barrel racing." Ginny Morgan scowled at the mare pulling away from her. "And I'll be damned if I can see her making much of a cutting horse or cow pony."

"She'll make a lovely riding animal. She's got a perfect lope and is so gentle a child could handle her."

"So…a pet?" Ginny's scowl turned to a sneer. "Hell's bells, Jessi, I'm not in the business of keeping pets."

"How much?" Jessi faced her squarely even as the rashness of buying another horse filtered into reality. Her father had been complaining she was making them horse poor.

"Oh, take the damn thing! I don't know who besides a softhearted fool like you would want her."

She threw the reins at Jessi and strode off into the crowd.

What a witch! Too much money and too little heart. Now to find out about Ross.

Caught in the crowd intent on leaving the rodeo ground with the day's events ending, Jessi realized it would take her a long time to get to the first-aid trailer leading a nervous horse. Turning, she headed back to the stables. She'd leave Maisy in the barn while she went to inquire about Ross.

Once she'd settled the mare in her stall, she headed off at a jog through the thinning crowd, toward the medical facility. An ambulance, lights flashing, siren setting up a scream, was pulling away as she arrived.

"Ross Turner?" She pointed at the vehicle maneuvering out of the rodeo grounds.

"Yes." A young paramedic watching beside her nodded.

"How is he?"

"Sorry. We're not allowed to give out information to anyone other than family members. Not his sister, are you?"

"No, but his family and mine—"

"That doesn't qualify you to receive patient information. Sorry." He turned and walked back inside the facility.

Damn! I have to find out how Ross is. Mom and Dad will want to know… Of course—Clint!

Her fiancé, saddle bronc rider Clint Harrison, would have information on how badly Ross had been injured. They'd been competitors together at any number of rodeos over the years. When one of the riders was injured, news traveled fast among them. She headed off to find him.

Clint didn't know she was at the rodeo. Planning to surprise him with her unexpected arrival that evening, she'd learned the location of his trailer. She shoved that plan aside in favor of moving the surprise up a few hours. Finding out about Ross took precedence.

Arriving at Clint's big silver trailer parked near the back of the rodeo grounds, she didn't stop to knock. They'd been engaged for over a month, after all. No need for formalities. She pulled the door open…and froze.

Locked in a passionate embrace were the man she was planning to marry and Ginny Morgan. Clint was bare-chested. Ginny wore only a lacy black bra above hipster jeans. They pulled apart as the door opened.

"Good God, Jess, have you never learned to knock?" Ginny threw the words at her.

"Honey, it's not what it looks like…" Clint backed away from the woman and threw up his hands.

"Oh, for God's sake, Clint, she's not that stupid." Ginny grabbed up her shirt and thrust her arms into the sleeves. "It's about time she woke up and smelled the roses. You rodeo cowboys are all about as faithful as tomcats. She's been around the circuit long enough to know the score."

Ginny's words snapped Jessi back to mobility. She whirled and bolted out of the trailer. Blinded by anger and pain, she ran, stumbling, toward the barn. She had to get home…fast.

Damn him, damn him, damn him!

Her heart banging at her ribs, she burst into Maisy's stall, causing the little mare to lurch away from her.

"Stop it, just stop it, Maisy!" Pain and anger sapping her usual patience, she snapped a lead onto the mare's halter. With long strides fueled by outrage, the skittish mare prancing behind her, she headed for her horse trailer.

Two-timing bastard! I hope the next bronc he rides tosses him so far he'll be in the land of stars and stripes when he touches down!

"Hey, babe." The two-timing bastard himself came running after her. His wet shirt hung open over a broad, well-muscled chest. When he caught up to her, he tried to take her into his arms, but she shoved him back.

"Get away from me, Clint." Anger, hard and brutal,

choked up in the back of her throat and made it difficult for her to speak. Her hands clenched into fists. "Don't ever touch me again!"

"Okay, okay." He threw up his hands, causing the mare to shy and dance.

Shoving him aside, she led Maisy into the trailer, tied her, and fastened the butt chain. When she emerged, he was waiting.

"Jess, honey." He plastered his most irresistible grin across his handsome, weathered face. "Come on, baby. This isn't worth fightin' over."

"Get out of my way!" Her words barked out as he tried to block her. "Go find Ginny!"

"Listen, honey…" He strode beside her as she walked to the truck's cab. "What you saw back there didn't mean anything. You know Ginny. Always up for a bit of fun."

"Fun, is that what you call it?" She clamped her hand on the truck's door handle. "Fun for a man engaged to be married this fall? Come on, Clint! I'm not a complete idiot!"

"Of course you aren't, babe." His hand covered hers, stopping it from opening the door. "I love you. You know that. Ginny caught me fresh out of the shower, that's all."

"Oh, and that's why your arms were around her, and why she had her shirt off? Why your hair was bone dry?" She glared at him through the rain.

"What can I say? She's one brazen hussy." The roguish grin widened.

"And you're one two-timing bastard!" She wrenched free and pulled open the driver's door. "Get away from me, Clint, before I'm tempted to run you over."

"Okay, okay." Again he held up his hands. This time he backed off. "But you haven't seen the last of me, baby, not by a long shot. As soon as I'm finished on the circuit, I'll be back courtin' you hot and heavy."

"Don't bother!" She slammed the door, turned the key in the ignition, and revved the motor.

As she swung out of the parking lot, she glanced into the rearview mirror and saw him standing with his hands on his hips, drenched in the downpour, watching her drive away.

Idiot! If he thinks he'll find me waiting in September, he has one big surprise in store.

With a knife-sharp pain stabbing body and soul, Jessi nevertheless knew she had to find out all she could about Ross Turner before she headed home. Her mother and father would want to know. Furthermore, she liked Ross…what she could remember of him.

But, oh, God, all I want to do is curl up in a ball and forget what I saw. I swear I'll never leave myself open to this kind of hurt ever again.

At the entrance to the rodeo grounds, she stopped for the gate to be opened by Bossy, the elderly man who'd been on duty there for all equine events for as long as she could remember.

"What's the news on Ross?" She wound down the window to ask as he limped out of his small shelter. Bossy had the scoop on anything that happened in and around the arena.

"He must be still breathin'." He came to lean on the driver's door and squint in at her. "The ambulance took off out of here so fast I barely had time to open the gate."

"That's positive." She struggled to sound normal and ignore the trembling in her sweating hands. Clint's betrayal had to be put on a backburner. Ross's fate was her main concern. It was a life-and-death situation. If only the image of Clint and Ginny in each other's arms wouldn't keep rising up to blur everything else that had happened that day and prevent her from putting events in proper prospective.

"Yeah, well, Ross was due to take a fall. He's had a horseshoe up his ass for years, if you ask me. Never a bad accident, always in the money. Maybe it's time for him to quit while he still has a chance at a healthy life ahead of him…if it isn't already too late. I reckon your folks will be right concerned, what with them and the Turners being great friends."

"Yes, no doubt." Bossy knew everything about everyone's life who was a regular in the equine events. "Thanks, Bossy. I'd better hit the trail."

As Bossy stepped away from the truck, she wound up the window and shifted into drive. It was a good two hours' journey to her parents' ranch. She couldn't wait to get there. As soon as she arrived, she'd saddle Maisy and take a lope across the meadows and up into the birches. She needed time to collect her thoughts and emotions before she faced her mother and father and had to tell them double bad news.

She'd talk about Ross first. Later, when she had a chance to be alone with her mother, she'd tell her about Clint. Joan Wallace would take the news better than her husband. Jack Wallace had been counting on Clint to join them on their ranch after the wedding and ease his way into the business as his son-in-law. Now…

An arctic chill engulfed her heart as a conversation

she'd overheard in a restaurant near the rodeo grounds two days ago flashed back across her mind.

"Yeah, old Clint's making his bed really comfy cozy," she'd heard from the booth behind the one in which she was waiting for her fiancé. "He knows he's gettin' too dinged up for the rodeo circuit. Marryin' Jack Wallace's daughter will give him a nice, soft place to land. With that girl as his only child, Jack will welcome an experienced cowboy marryin' his daughter and takin' over the ranch when he gets too old to do it himself. Yeah, yeah, that Clint is no dumb bunny, for all the times he got tossed on his head and backside."

She'd shrugged it off at the time. Cowboy gossip. Clint loved her, wanted to spend the rest of his life with her. Now it all seemed far too believable.

She sucked in a deep breath. Oh, God, what a day! If she didn't love ranch life and have to accept the fact that cowboys were part of it, she'd want to leave the whole thing behind. Staring out through the driving rain, she wished the slashing windshield wipers could also clear away the tears that had begun to trickle down her cheeks.

****

"Honey, I'm so sorry…so very, very sorry." Joan Wallace sat on the edge of Jessi's bed in her room upstairs in the rambling log ranch house. "I never would have thought Clint would do such a thing. And with Ginny Morgan, the queen of spoiled brats, not even one of us"—Jessie knew "us" meant ranchers—"but the daughter of an oil man."

"Mom, let's wait a while before we tell Dad. Right now, he's got enough to handle, what with Ross's accident."

10

Jessi was calm, in control. She'd shed her tears and initial outrage during the drive back to the ranch and the half-hour's ride aboard Maisy before talking to her mother. As she'd ridden back to the ranch, a bitter resolve as hard and cold as a January frost had settled over her. She'd never let herself be hurt like that again. Never, never, never.

"You're right." Joan put her hand over her daughter's. "We'll be heading for the hospital to be with Bob and Laura as soon as he finishes up with the stock. I know you can manage things here. Thank God Chase and Janice are on their parents' ranch to take care of things while they're with Ross. There's no telling how long Bob and Laura will be needed at the hospital."

"Yes, the Turners are fortunate to have two sons, even if the second hasn't been much support to the family...always off rodeoing." Jessi, not for the first time that day, felt a twinge as she knew what the loss of Clint would mean to the future of her family's ranch. "Chase has always kicked in to help his dad, to let him know he'll handle the reins when the time comes."

"Now, Jessi, don't go there." Her mother was quick to catch her up. "Neither your father nor I would want you to marry simply to provide this ranch with someone to take over. That would be medieval, wouldn't it?" Joan Wallace smiled at her. "Furthermore, we both know you're perfectly capable of running this place on your own."

"I guess." She forced herself to smile back, even though she knew it was a weak imitation of the real thing.

"Now, if you're sure you'll be all right, I'm going

to change into fresh clothes and meet your dad at the truck for the drive to the hospital." Joan stood and pushed up the sleeves of her plaid shirt. In jeans that covered slim hips, she looked more like Jessi's older sister than her mother. Jessi admired her.

"Sure, I'll be fine. You go. The Turners will appreciate your company."

After her mother had gone, she gazed out her upstairs bedroom window. The rain had stopped before she'd gotten to the ranch, allowing her to have a dry ride aboard Maisy. Now, an evening rainbow bowed over the foothills.

Maybe it's a sign of brighter days ahead.

She went downstairs and out to the barn. There was always work to do. Maybe it would help to wash away some of the terrible images of the day.

Once inside, amid the familiar sights, sounds, and smells of horses, Jessi heaved a sigh. She was home...home where she belonged, where she would always belong.

A sniffling from the stall to her left drew her attention.

"Badger." The old buckskin was thrusting his whiskered nose toward her. "Good to see you, guy. You've always been the best...strong and loyal and hardworking." She leaned her forehead against his neck. "Too bad some people wouldn't take an example from you."

Badger blew softly and pressed against her.

As she picked up a manure fork and headed into his stall, she knew one thing for certain. She'd never again get involved with another rodeo cowboy.

Chapter Two

Ross Turner stared out the window of his room at the Calgary rehab center, the bleakness that had settled in his gut over the past six weeks bringing him near vomiting again. There was nothing left for him. The doctors had told him his bull-riding days were over, that one more spill would see him permanently in a wheelchair. Rodeo had been his way of life. He couldn't imagine doing anything else. He gripped the cane in his hand until his knuckles whitened.

"Ross, honey!" His mother burst into his room, followed by his tall, barrel-chested father. "How are you doing today?" She flew across the room to put her hands on his arms and stand on tiptoes to plant a kiss on his cheek.

"Fine, Mom, just fine." He loved his parents and didn't want to cause them any further worry. "How are you, Dad?"

"Doing well, son." The big rancher, a wide grin on his face, joined his wife to slap his son on the back. "We've been hearing good things from your doctor. He says you're being released tomorrow. We'll be here to pick you up at noon and take you back to the ranch."

"Thanks, Dad, but that won't be necessary." Ross struggled for the courage to tell his parents his plan. "I'm going to New Brunswick...to your old family farm on Chaleur Bay. I've got a plane ticket."

"Ross…" His mother stared at him, eyes wide. She looked, Ross thought, as if he'd just told her he was going to Mars. "No. Surely you're joking. You can't possibly be considering going to live on that dilapidated place. No one has lived in the house for years!"

"Mom, understand. I don't want to go home to be a burden to you and Dad."

"But, Ross…"

He struggled to ignore the pleading, the lack of comprehension in his mother's eyes. He loved the woman, but sometimes she could be smothering in her concern.

"Laura, let the lad be." Bob Turner stepped away from his son and drew his wife with him. "He needs to get away on his own to prove himself, to be satisfied he can manage. Isn't that right, son?"

"Yeah." The word came out softly. It was enough for his parents to understand his decision on that basis.

"Ross." His name from his mother's lips was so quiet, so filled with apprehension, he had to fight to keep his resolve.

"Sorry, Mom. I'll be back once I get feeling like myself again. For Christmas, for sure."

"Christmas! That's months away!"

"Come on, Laura. Kiss the boy goodbye and let's go. We have work at the ranch, and I'm sure he's got arrangements to make. Good luck, son." Bob Turner held out a hand to him.

Ross had to admit he was glad when they'd gone. Telling them his plans and watching his mother's agony of disappointment had almost made him cave. He had to get away, and not just, as his father had perceived, to prove himself. He had to get as far away from people who knew him, who might pity him or see him as a has-been, as possible. He'd been the best in the business. Now he was stumping along with a cane. He returned to staring out the window. That old farm in New Brunswick, thousands of miles away, seemed exactly the place he needed to be, at least for a while.

"Ross, baby!" Cat Holt's voice made him turn to face the tall, slender, dark-haired woman entering his room. She wore jeans that might have been painted on and a flame-red tank top that left little to the imagination. "I was in the neighborhood and thought I'd stop by to see how you're doing." She moved across the room, hips swaying, waist-length hair shining like a raven's wing. Pausing in front of him, she took him into her arms and pressed her lips to his.

Nothing. The word flashed into his mind. *Definitely nothing. Good God, is my love life over, too?*

"Nice of you to drop by...*now*, Cat." His response came out in a sarcastic drawl. "I've been here for weeks."

"I know, I know, baby, but I've been on the circuit...barrel racing, keeping pace."

Keeping pace...I just bet. With everything male that takes your fancy.

"So how are you doing?" She stepped back from him and pressed her question.

"Coming along just fine, Cat. Doctors say I'll be back in action next spring, maybe even midwinter on the southern circuit." Something, a mixture of pride and anger at her lack of previous concern, made him lie.

"Well, now, isn't that just great?" She tossed him a saucy, provocative glance. "And"—she stepped close once more and ran a finger down his chest to the top of his jeans—"all other channels working well?"

"Right as rain…as far as a man can tell in one of these places."

"Let me know the minute you're released, and we'll check that out, baby." Her brown eyes glinted seductively.

"Actually, I'm getting out tomorrow."

"Well, then, party time tomorrow night, baby. I'll book us a room and buy champagne. This calls for an all-out celebration."

"Sounds good, Cat, but it will have to wait. I'm heading to New Brunswick to visit the family farm."

"Why in hell would you do something like that?" She stepped back, astonishment in her expression.

"Because I need a little breathing space."

"Okay." She backed toward the door. "But keep in touch. Text me. Let me know the minute you're back in town."

"Sure. See you, Cat."

"See you, baby."

He watched as she waved from the doorway, then vanished down the hall. Her visit hadn't surprised him all that much, even though she hadn't been around for months.

Cat Holt worked with Simon Shoeman, one of the top promoters in the rodeo business. Ross didn't for a minute doubt Simon had sent Cat to see when one of his star attractions would be back to work, back to being a moneymaker at the box offices. Simon was a smooth operator. He would have reasoned that sending the sexy Cat would do more to lure Ross back to work than his visiting the bull rider.

Well, he'd given her an earful, hadn't he. Back to

work this winter! As if that was going to happen. Right now, all he wanted to do was catch that plane to New Brunswick and hermit himself away on that deserted farm with a truckload of liquor and no plans for the rest of his life.

****

As the Air Canada plane canted down toward the airport in Moncton, New Brunswick, Ross fastened his seatbelt and, not for the first time since leaving Calgary, had qualms about the wisdom of what he was doing. His Stetson had barely attracted a nod until he'd landed in Montreal. From there on, it had made him an oddity, a fish out of water, a cowboy out of the west. He'd stowed it in the luggage rack, but still he had the feeling fellow passengers were branding him as an anomaly. He definitely didn't feel at home among these easterners. Maybe he'd been crazy to come.

But it was too late to be having second thoughts now. The plane touched down with a jerk that always gave his gut a twitch. Riding a bull was nothing like landing in a huge junk of metal carrying God only knew how many gallons of flammable fuel. Ross Turner was definitely out of his element.

****

He felt even more displaced when he drove a rented 4x4 king cab into the overgrown dooryard of the Turner farm and braked to a stop. The house, barn, and a few scattered outbuildings, weathered gray and sagging, looked as if they'd been deserted for ages.

Probably infested with mice, if nothing worse. What the hell. I'm here and I'm going to stay...for a while.

He climbed out of the pickup's cab and searched

through the keys on his ring for the one his father had given him years ago when Bob Turner had inherited the property.

"Here, son," he'd said. "Maybe you'll want to go to New Brunswick some day. Take it. The key is probably worth more than the place. Your great-uncle lived there twenty years ago. Since then it's been deserted. Probably been vandalized to hell."

Well, at least that last didn't seem to be the case. The windows still had glass and no graffiti marred the cedar shingles. Damned place was so isolated vandals couldn't find it, he thought as he remembered the trek down the rutted, potholed road over which he'd just driven.

Grasping his cane, he headed around to the front of the house and looked out over Chaleur Bay. In the muggy, gray late summer day it lay flat and still. No life anywhere. A slight noise from the verandah made him turn. A dog, not much bigger than a large beagle, matted red coat full of burrs, stood at the top of the steps. So thin she resembled a skeleton with a dirty rug thrown over it, she was staring at him as she stood on wobbly legs.

"Jesus!" Ross started slowly toward her. "Hello, girl. It is 'girl,' isn't it? You all alone out here?"

When he arrived at the steps, he sat down with his back to her. He knew better than to try to force his attentions on a strange animal. "You look as if you could use a square meal," he said, avoiding a direct look at her. "I'm going to cook a steak once I get settled in. How about sharing it with me?"

He waited and finally he felt a hot, dry little snout against his neck, sniffing, checking him out. Again he waited. Only when she'd finished her inspection did he get slowly to his feet and continue on up the steps. She followed, stumbling on the top one. He resisted the urge to help her. She had her pride…just like he had his.

He inserted the key in the lock, and after a few cranks, it gave. The door swung open to emit a gush of stale, musty air. Stepping into the shadowy interior, he looked around as dust motes, aroused by his entrance, swirled.

Time had stood still in the place. From scuffed hardwood floors to peeling wallpaper, an ambience of early twentieth-century pervaded the interior. Glancing to his right, he saw a shabby parlor with faded, threadbare Victorian furniture. Ragged draperies covered a window that faced out toward the bay. He tightened his lips and headed down the dark corridor toward the back of the house.

"May as well take it all in at once, girl," he said to the dog that followed close at his heels. "Like pulling off a Band-Aid."

Pausing in the kitchen doorway, he looked around at a big rusted cooking stove, cupboards that had once been painted green but now had mostly peeled back to their original wood tones, and a dirty enamel sink with taps mounted high on a stained backboard.

He turned a tap. No water. Of course. He'd have to have the electricity turned on and then see if he could find a pump somewhere, either in a cupboard in the house or in some kind of cave under it, and prime it.

He stepped out onto the back porch and saw a hand pump to the left. Farther back in the field stood a canted outhouse.

"All this might not bother you"—he looked down

at the dog—"but I'm sure as hell not into roughing it to this degree. First thing tomorrow we get a plumber out here and a bathroom installed."

She looked up at him, round eyes gaunt.

"Okay, first to more immediate concerns." He limped down the steps and around to the cargo space of his truck. He removed a camp stove with a propane tank, a grocery bag, and a case of beer. "Come on, girl. Let's set up camp on the front verandah. I'm thinking you wouldn't object to a nice, juicy streak. You probably need a drink, too, but I don't think a Bud is your thing. With a bit of water from the bay, I should be able to get that hand pump going. There must be a bowl somewhere in that monstrosity of a house that will suit your needs."

Chapter Three

Jessi paused in lunging a bay gelding to watch the maroon king cab heading up the road toward the ranch. She recognized the Turners' vehicle. As it came closer, she saw Laura Turner at the wheel. She was alone. The woman stopped beside the paddock where Jessi stood and got out.

"Good morning, Jessi." Laura smiled, swinging out and striding over to the fence. "Beautiful day. Lovely beginning to the fall, isn't it?"

"It surely is." Jessi freed the gelding and walked over to join the woman. "Hard to believe it's September already. The summer flew."

"Yes, well, for some of us." Laura Turner looked down at her boots, and Jessi was immediately sorry for what she'd said. It must have been a long three months for the Turners, traveling first to the hospital to visit Ross and then to the rehab center where he'd spent several weeks.

"Sorry, Laura. I know it's been a difficult time for you and your family. How is Ross doing?"

"Physically a good deal better, his doctor told me." She paused and gripped the top rail of the fence in both hands. "Mentally and emotionally…"

"I'm sorry to hear it. Is there anything we can do to help? Mom, Dad, or myself? You know we're only too willing…"

"As a matter of fact, that's why I'm here." She looked squarely at Jessi. "Jess, I'd like you to use your healing skills to help Ross."

"*My* healing skills?" The woman's words caught Jessi completely off guard. "I work with horses, not people."

"But you identify with both. You've often told me you've seen problems as being with the rider, not the horse. That's what Ross needs right now. Someone who understands the relationship between animals and human beings and how to deal with the situation when things go wrong between them."

"Laura…"

"Jessi, I know how busy you are here at the ranch and, believe me, I wouldn't ask if I weren't desperate. Ross took off for New Brunswick to live in an old farmhouse that belongs to Bob's family. No one has lived in it for years. I can't imagine its present condition. Ross is determined to hermit himself away, to give up on life."

"But why? Lots of rodeo cowboys heal up and go back at it, maybe not bull riding, but…"

"The doctors have told him he'll never do that kind of strenuous riding again. They've told him he has to retire from the ring or his next fall will cripple him for life."

"Oh."

"Yes, oh. Jessi, I'm afraid for Ross, afraid of what will become of him if he doesn't wake up and realize there's life after bull riding. You've made horses recover from accidents. I remember what you did for our stallion, the Grey Gent, after he got onto the road and was struck by a truck. Work your magic on Ross."

"Laura, the Grey Gent is a horse. Ross is a human being."

"But you brought the Gent back to life, Jessi. That beautiful animal would have withered away in a corner of the pasture if you hadn't managed to revive his confidence and courage. That's what Ross needs right now—someone to get him back on his feet, to convince him there's more to life than being a rodeo superstar."

The pleading in Laura Turner's blue eyes caught at Jessi's heart. The woman was her mother's best friend. If the tables were turned, Joan Wallace would have expected Ross to try to help Jessi.

"It will be roundup time in October." She tried a feeble protest. "Mom and Dad need every rider they can get..."

"I'll send over as many men as they need." She stood looking the young woman squarely in the face. "Jessi..." Her tone softened. "I know what happened between you and Clint Harrison. Maybe getting away for a while..."

Oh, God, does everyone know what a fool the man made of me, of our relationship?

"Over and done with." She struggled to sound casual. "But how did you hear about it? I only told Mom and Dad, and they haven't been spreading the news. Has Clint been shooting off his mouth?" Annoyance darkened the last sentence.

"Not that I'm aware. I know only because Bob asked your dad when the wedding was to be...before or after roundup...so we could make plans. Bob said that, from your father's response, he wouldn't want to be Clint Harrison—or if he was, he wouldn't come within a hundred miles of Jack Wallace."

23

"Yes, well, Dad can be a tad protective." She forced a weak grin. "Give me a few days, Laura. I'll talk to Mom and Dad and let you know."

****

Jessi stepped out onto the verandah of her parents' ranch house and drew in a deep breath of late summer morning air. The sun, peeking over the foothills, bathed the shorn hayfields in its light, turning the gravel road that led toward town into a blinding yellow glare.

Good morning for a gallop.

But that would have to wait. She went down the steps and headed for the barn. There was work to do. She had horses to feed and train, stalls to muck out, and hopefully some time left to help her parents with their ranch work. Always lots to do, always lots to, mostly, keep her from thinking about Clint Harrison and ignoring his barrage of calls and texts. She'd been relieved a couple of days earlier when they'd suddenly, finally, stopped.

She entered the barn and paused at Badger's stall to rub the nose he thrust out at her.

"Good morning, boy." She grinned. "Always up with the crows, aren't you?"

"I was up way before that." Something jumped in her chest as she whirled to find Clint Harrison entering the barn, grinning at her. "I've been waitin' out by the round pen for near an hour."

"Clint! What are you doing here?" Surprised to see him, she gasped out the words.

"You weren't answering my texts or calls." He reached to take her into his arms, but she dodged away. "So I decided to stop by. Come on, baby, don't be like that." He tried to embrace her again, but she shrugged him off. "You're not going to let a little harmless fun with Ginny Morgan ruin what we had."

"A little harmless fun! Is that what you call it?" Coming out of the shock of seeing him, Jessi went into fighting mode. "Clint, we were engaged to be married. I'd say that made our relationship exclusive. Apparently you didn't see it that way." Her initial outrage at his appearance cooling to cold, hard bitterness, she faced him, hands on her hips. "Actually, I'm glad it happened." She narrowed her eyes and felt the planes of her face tightening as she continued. "It saved me from being tied up with a man with all the moral fiber of a tomcat."

"Jessi, come on. Do you think Ginny Morgan could be seriously interested in a rodeo cowboy? Hell, she's a multi-millionaire's daughter. Matter of fact, she got herself engaged to a guy from Texas last month…oil, cattle, you name it, he's into it."

"Oh, so I was the best you thought you could do financially?" His words whipped like a high wind onto her ire. "Those cowboys I overheard talking in the restaurant were right. I was just a ticket to a comfortable future."

"Damn it, Jess, I don't know what you heard while you were eavesdropping, but…"

"I wasn't eavesdropping! I have more integrity than to be guilty of that deviousness."

"Now, look here, honey. We had a good thing goin'. Come here and let me remind you." This time a quick move gave him success in grabbing her.

"Let me go, Clint!" She struggled in his powerful grasp.

"Yes, let her go." The bronc rider's hands released

her as he swung to face the steely grim face of Jack Wallace. The big man advanced toward the couple, a powerful dark silhouette with sunlight at his back.

"Jack! Good to see you, man." Clint instantly became the affable good ol' boy as he advanced toward Jessi's father, hand extended. "Just dropped by to see my girl."

"Well, now you've seen *my* girl, so you'd better be going." In his youth, Jack Wallace had been a bulldogger at rodeos, an event that saw the biggest, most powerful men compete. He'd lost little of that stature over the years. Now he was a commanding presence that even a man like Clint Harrison wasn't eager to challenge.

"No need." Clint kept up the farce even as the other man refused his hand and he had to let it drop back to his side. "I have a couple of days off. I thought I'd hang my hat here and help out around the place. Good to get familiar with it. After Jessi and I are married…"

"They'll be having snowball fights in hell by the time that happens, if I have anything to say about it." Jack Wallace stepped closer to him. "Now get, before I decide to boot your sorry behind so hard you'll land in the good old U.S. of A."

During the confrontation, Clint had swung around so that his back was to Badger's stall. As if on cue, the old gelding lunged out with his snout and rammed the man in the back. He was plummeted into Jack Wallace's wide chest, then seized by big hands and expelled from the barn so forcefully he fell to his knees, Stetson flying from his head.

"I see you parked your truck down the road a ways." Jack Wallace followed him to the doorway.

"Get your ass into it and the hell off my property."

"Okay, okay, Jack." Clint Harrison stumbled to his feet, grabbing up his Stetson. He banged it against his dusty jeans before slapping it back onto his head. "But you haven't seen the last of me, not by a long shot. Jessi loves me. Once she's had time to come to her senses, she'll be glad to hook up with me again."

Limping, he headed down the road out of the ranch yard toward his truck that Jessi hadn't noticed in the glare of the rising sun.

"Thanks, Dad." Jessi came to stand by her father and watch the man leave.

"Not a problem, honey." Jack Wallace put an arm about his daughter's slim shoulders and gave her a squeeze. He grinned down at her. "Now that we've got rid of one pile of manure, I think it's time we tackled some more honest stuff." He released her and handed her a pitchfork.

As Jessi Wallace began to muck out a stall, she came to a decision. She paused, pulled out her cell and made the call. She didn't want to chance another encounter with Clint Harrison, one when her father wasn't around.

"Laura? Jessi here. I've decided to go to New Brunswick."

"Jessi, that's wonderful!" Laura Turner's delight at her acceptance bubbled over the phone. "And more good news. Bob tells me there's a horse-breeding facility and riding school not far from the farm. It's run by a Dr. Shelby Masters, a veterinarian. I'm thinking you might want to get in contact with her…just so you won't feel isolated with Ross in his present depressed mood. I've heard good things about this woman and her work with horses. Maybe you two can team up. At the very least, you'll be able to borrow one of her animals and go riding."

"So you've already scouted out the territory for me?" Jessi couldn't stop the small grin starting at the corners of her mouth. "You must have been pretty confident I'd eventually cave and go."

"I must admit I was." The woman's tone softened. "You're a good woman, Jessi Wallace. I've never seen you turn down any animal…or person…in need. Most sincerely, thank you."

What have I gotten myself into? As Jessi accepted the woman's gratitude, misgivings flooded through her. *Offering to help the rock star of rodeo get his groove back. I have to be crazy…and desperate to get away.*

****

"You did the right thing, honey." Joan Wallace sat across the kitchen table from her daughter in the century-old ranch house kitchen. "You remember that winter when you were ten and your dad got hurt? Bob and his sons drove over every morning to help. Fifty miles is a considerable distance on these roads in January."

"I remember." Jessi stared down into her coffee cup. "But, Mom, I don't see how I can help Ross if doctors weren't able to. He needs a physiotherapist or a psychologist, or maybe both. I deal with injured and traumatized horses."

"We're all God's creatures." Joan stood and went to the counter to replenish her cup. "Misgivings and lost confidence are common to all of us. Do what you'd normally do to restore an ailing spirit. Follow your instincts. You'll be fine. And furthermore…"

"Furthermore what, Mom?" Jessi looked sharply over at her mother.

"Furthermore, the rodeo circuit will be wrapping up soon." She didn't have to continue. Jessi caught her drift.

"And you assume Clint will be back…again and again?"

"Well, honey, of all the things Clint might be, he's no quitter. I don't for a minute believe he's going to give you up easily."

"I'll start packing."

****

Two days later Jessi Wallace sat on a flight headed for Moncton, New Brunswick. It had been a prolonged journey, with a major layover in Montreal that would make her arrival in the Maritime province late evening. And then, according to Bob Turner's best recollection of a visit to the farm years ago, it was a three-hour drive to the old homestead. So she'd be driving through strange country in darkness. *Great.*

She opened the equine magazine she'd bought to read during the flight, but found herself distracted. Her thoughts kept going to the man she was being sent to help.

It seemed incredible to her that the Ross Turner she knew, albeit mainly by reputation these past few years, had become an embittered recluse. When she'd known him ten years ago, he'd been a good-natured, fun-loving, devil-may-care type. Later, when he'd joined the rodeo circuit and become a successful bull rider, she recalled seeing photos of him winning the event in various newspapers and western magazines. He'd always been good-looking, but over the years, unless those pictures lied, he'd become one handsome hunk, suitable for the cover of a romance novel. This fact, combined with a charismatic personality she'd heard him demonstrate on various television interviews, had earned him the moniker "the rock star of rodeo."

Now she, Jessi Wallace, rancher's daughter and horse trainer, had been called in to help the man. And from what his mother had indicated, it was the last thing Ross Turner wanted. *Incredible!*

"Please fasten your seatbelts," announced the flight attendant's voice over the PA system. "We're heading into minor turbulence."

With a sigh, Jessi moved to comply.

I'm probably heading into major turbulence…at ground level. If Ross Turner is determined to become a recluse, I'll be about as welcome as a burr under a saddle.

****

That must be Rogersville up ahead. Good lord, what a terrible night!

Through rain and fog, Jessi Wallace saw the lights of a settlement come into view. The number of miles she'd driven from the Moncton Airport indicated on her GPS that she should be entering the small, rural community. The long, dark stretch of highway she'd been traveling had given little evidence of human habitation aside from a few lights beaming out from well-spaced houses along the road. Not normally one to give in to trepidations, Jessi Wallace was nevertheless thousands of miles from her home and alone in the stormy night.

Better gas up. According to these directions I'm still at least fifty miles from Carleton, the nearest town to Ross's family farm. Then, if the directions Bob and Laura gave me are right on, it's another fifteen miles or so out along the coast.

Having no desire to get stranded in the inhospitable night, she pulled into a gas bar that offered full service. A man wearing a sou'wester dashed out to greet her.

"Fill it up, please," she called through a window she'd cracked enough to speak to the attendant.

"Sure thing."

She sat and waited while he filled the tank, then rolled the window far enough to accept the debit machine he held out to her.

"Goin' far?" he asked as she inserted the card and punched in her code.

"Far enough. To Carleton and about fifteen miles down the coast beyond."

"Not the night for that, miss." The middle-aged face trimmed with gray stubble frowned down at her. "Hear they're gettin' a whale of a storm up that way. Tail end of a hurricane that blew up the coast. We get a fair bunch of them this time of year."

"Thanks for the information. I'll manage." She retrieved her card, smiled at him, and rolled up her window.

Just what I need. A hurricane.

Thank goodness she'd had the foresight to rent a four-wheel-drive Jeep at the airport. Even if the road leading to Ross's remote farmhouse was a sea of mud, it should make it through.

Jessi adjusted her hands on the steering wheel and told herself again she'd had no choice about making this trip.

"Make him want to live again, Jessi." His mother's

last words to her echoed in her head as she drove down the lonely stretch of New Brunswick highway. "If anyone can, it's you. I've seen you with horses. You've got a gift for reviving the *joie de vivre*. Who knows?" she'd continued, her words brightening with hopeful innuendo. "You might even get to like each other. It can be very romantic along New Brunswick's northeast coast."

A smirk jerked up one corner of her mouth. There was no power on earth that could make her get interested in Ross Turner on a personal level. Handsome rodeo cowboys wouldn't be on her radar for a very long time…if ever. There wasn't a New Brunswick beachfront romantic enough to make her fall for another one of those types.

For the next hour she drove through what seemed like an endless tunnel of rain-slickened asphalt and night-blackened forest. She could easily have counted the few vehicles she encountered.

When a roadside sign informed her Carleton, the town nearest the Turner farm, was ten kilometers ahead, she heaved a sigh. Shortly, multiple lights brightening the night told her she was entering the community. After fighting this tropical-type downpour and buffeting wind, she'd be glad to reach her destination no matter how Ross Turner chose to welcome her. "Any port in a storm" flashed across her mind.

****

She stopped at a take-out restaurant in Carleton and ran inside, head ducked against the driving wind and rain. Laura had given her directions from the town to the farm, but she wanted to confirm them with some of the locals. Ross's mother had never been to New

Brunswick.

"Hi, I'm looking for directions to the Turner farm." She smiled at the young girl behind the cash register. "It's out along the coast road."

She looked blankly at Jessi. "Sorry. Never heard of it."

"I have." An older man who'd been working the grill came forward. "You keep right on this road, young lady. It'll take you out along the shore. Watch your mileage. The Turner farm should be fifteen miles from here, on your left. The road is pretty overgrown, and the old sign board is hanging by a single nail, but you should be able to find it."

"Thank you." She turned to leave.

"Maybe you should take a place here in town for the night." His words stopped her. "I hear the shore road is bad right now. Waves going over it in places. The police will likely be closing it soon. They do in most storms like this one."

"I'll manage." She smiled her thanks and headed back to her vehicle.

****

That guy wasn't exaggerating. What a night! What a road! What a storm!

Wind yanked at the vehicle as water gushed across the road in cascades. Several times, waves rose above the bank of the bay and hurtled in front of her, blinding her in a hard, white sheet.

Good God, how much farther?

The dial on her dashboard informed her she'd driven fifteen miles from the restaurant. Jessi slowed the Jeep. Squinting through the driving rain, she saw a faded sign hanging sideways on a single nail as it flapped in the wind. It read "Turner Farm." She braked to a stop and perused the two water-filled tire ruts leading into a thick, dark coniferous forest.

It was like the entrance to an eerie, mysterious estate in one of those gothic novels her grandmother had left in the attic and which her mother still read during long winter evenings. Jessi had to admit she'd enjoyed a few herself, but this wasn't a bit of dated fiction. It was miserable reality.

Laura's son definitely knew how to choose a place to hide out. With a sigh of resignation, she eased her foot off the brake and turned the Jeep into the lane.

She'd gone what she estimated to be a half mile when the trail swerved and canted to the right. As the beams of her headlights swung around the bend, her breath caught in her throat. A huge fallen pine, its branches sticking up higher than her vehicle's roof, blocked the trail.

Slamming her foot down on the brake pedal, she felt the Jeep lurch and slide before swerving to a stop. Jessi was flung forward against her seatbelt. The vehicle halted, half its hood buried in the branches.

Briefly, shock held her immobile. Then, turning off the ignition, she rallied and took stock of her situation.

Not hurt but, hell and damnation, where did that tree come from? Just what I needed to top off this miserable day.

She released the seatbelt, unlocked the door, and leaving it open to keep the interior light on, stepped out into the bucketing rain to survey her situation.

It wasn't encouraging. Ducking back inside, she pulled out her cell and tried to place a call for roadside assistance. Not unexpectedly, all she got was static.

No cell towers in this backwoods, I suppose. Or maybe the storm has done a number on them. Well, no choice. I'll have to walk the rest of the way.

The prospect disheartened her. Tired, wet, and hungry, she needed rest, warmth, and food, not a midnight hike through a torrential downpour in unfamiliar territory.

She gave herself a mental shake. The grill attendant had said the cottage was only about a mile off the main road. She couldn't have that much farther to go. She picked up her purse.

No point in rummaging through my luggage for a raincoat. I'm already drenched. And to think I bought this suit to look businesslike and professional!

She slung the purse strap over one shoulder and across her chest, clambered out of the Jeep, and slammed the door shut. For a moment the intensity of the darkness blinded her. It was like being plummeted into a great, black, drenching hole.

Closing her eyes, she willed them to become accustomed to the darkness. When she opened them, she could discern what she hoped would be enough to keep her on the trail and out of the surrounding trees.

Here goes.

She locked the vehicle and headed down the rutted trail, head bent against wind and rain, stumbling over ruts and tree roots.

Chapter Four

Ross Turner took his third beer of the night out of the refrigerator. That appliance and a two-burner countertop electric stove were the only evidence of modernization in the dingy, dilapidated kitchen. He screwed off the long neck's cap and then, grasping his cane, limped to a battered wooden chair and dropped into it. The old, scarred pine table beside him was littered with dirty dishes and containers from take-out restaurants.

Damn, his leg hurt. Maybe this god-awful night had something to do with it. Or was he just getting old before his time, complaining how damp made his bones ache? He'd heard enough of the old-timers talk that way but hadn't expected to feel or sound like one at this age.

The gale, howling in off the bay, rattled the windows and shrieked down the chimney. The little dog he'd named Fox, because of her color, raised her head from where she was curled up beneath the table and looked up at him.

"Bugger of a night, right, girl? Well, at least now you're not out in it and hungry."

He dragged his chair closer to the warmth of the wood-burning cookstove and was glad he'd had the foresight to bring wood in from a pile by the barn before the storm struck. A pair of old oil lamps he'd found in a cupboard fortunately had been left full of fuel. Now one in the middle of the table and the other on the countertop afforded the only illumination in the room. He'd had electricity turned on shortly after he arrived, but the storm had apparently knocked it out of commission. All he had tonight were the lamps, their flickering shadows haunting the neglected farmhouse along with his thoughts and memories.

Mustn't open the fridge any more than necessary. Have to preserve what cold there is inside. In an effort to bring himself back to the moment and the practical, he recalled his mother's words of wisdom during power outages at the ranch.

He ran his thumb up and down the sweating long neck and thought about her phone call the previous day. She'd said she was sending someone to check up on him, someone who could help him recover.

Recover. As if it was as simple as getting over a bout of stomach flu. Didn't she realize his life would never be the same, that what he'd lived for, ever since he'd been a kid of sixteen, had been taken from him? Didn't she realize what limping around with a cane for the rest of his years would do to him? He loved the woman, but sometimes she just didn't understand him at all. Not like she understood Chase.

Chase. His perfect brother. He suppressed a guffaw. He loved the guy but, hell, he made it hard. Chase who'd gone to college, who'd gotten a degree in business administration to come back not only to help with the physical running of their parents' ranch but to make it a financial success. Chase who'd married Janet, a rancher's daughter from the Peace River District, pretty, clever, the all-around perfect mate for a man who had dedicated his life to cattle, horses, and the rangeland.

He got up and went to add wood to the stove. The effort it took annoyed him. Would nothing ever be easy again? Sinking back onto his chair, he grabbed his beer and quaffed it down.

Maybe he was right where he belonged. He looked out the window into the storm-blackened night. Maybe he'd stay here forever, become the crazy old hermit, a local legend. He fingered the stubble on his chin. He'd grow a beard, and each night he'd drink himself into oblivion on cheap whisky or homemade wine.

"Ross!" His name accompanied by a pounding at the door snapped him out of his thoughts.

"What the…?" He jolted upright on his chair and grabbed his cane.

"Ross Turner, let me in right now!"

A female voice. Fox jumped to her paws, a growl rumbling in her throat.

"Hang on, hang on. Take it easy, Fox." He got to his feet, stumped to the door, and pulled back the deadbolt.

A shaft of lightning accompanied a roll of thunder as a drenched woman tumbled inside. When she swung to glare up at him between long, rain-soaked planes of hair, her expression made the storm outside pale in ferocity.

"Jess? Jessi Wallace?" His astonishment couldn't have been more intense.

"What were you doing…sleeping? I was standing out there for…" She pushed past him into the kitchen.

"Jessi Wallace?" He shut the door after her.

"Stop repeating my name like a retarded parrot."

Anger belched out of every word. "I left home at four a.m. this morning, had a miserable flight from Calgary with lots of turbulence, and then a delay in Montreal, never mind the drive from Moncton to this God-forsaken place. I'm not in the mood to listen to you babbling my name and staring at me as if that last bolt of lightning had struck you."

"No, I can see you're not." Ross let his gaze roam over her dark blue outfit. "God, what's that you're wearing? You look like a social worker...a very wet social worker."

"It's called a pantsuit. Don't tell me you've never seen a woman wearing one?"

"I've never seen *you* wearing one."

"Well, considering how seldom we've met in the past ten years, that's no surprise." She glared up at him. "And I've never seen you looking like you do now, either."

She was staring him up and down, and he realized what she saw. A man with shaggy black hair curling below his ears and a scruffy beard shadowing his jaws and chin. A man wearing grubby jeans and the same rumpled chambray shirt he'd slept in for the last few days. A man who hadn't bothered to shower...recently. Behind him, a table littered with the empty containers of take-out food and a cupboard sporting an array of empty beer bottles. In the lanterns' light, the house must look like the den of a derelict.

I look—and smell—the right broken-down bum...in a perfect setting.

"Are you the faith healer my mother told me she was sending?" He pulled his thoughts away from his appearance and let the annoyance he was feeling reflect

39

into his remark.

Damn it, a family friend. Not someone a man could just throw out without a by-your-leave. Laura Turner, you've screwed me over this time, for sure and certain.

"I seriously doubt she used those words."

"Maybe not, but something to that effect." He reached past her for a jacket hanging on a peg near the door. "You'll have to stay the night. You must be nuts to have driven out here in this storm. I'll get your stuff and you can change out of that wet...pantsuit. Where did you park your vehicle?"

"About a half mile down the road." She swiped dripping hair back from her face.

"What?"

"There's a tree across your lane...a great big ol' pine. I had to walk the last half mile or so."

"Hell!" He withdrew his hand from the jacket and stepped back.

"Yeah, hell. Now, I'd be obliged if you'd lend me something to wear. I'm soaked to the skin."

"Do I have a choice?" His surprise at her appearance vanishing, his annoyance at his mother's sending Jessi Wallace—Jessi Wallace, who worked with injured horses—blossomed. "Down the hall to the right, you'll find a bathroom. Hanging on a peg behind the door, there's a robe. Don't try to shower. The power's out, so the water pump isn't working. I have to conserve what's in the tank."

"The perfect way to end this crazy day." Looking about as happy as a wet kitten and twice as belligerent, she glanced toward the black hallway.

"I'll need a light."

"Here, take this." He indicated the lamp on the

table.

"Thank you." The words mirrored her undiminished annoyance. She picked it up and, holding it aloft, headed off into the darkness.

Damn and double damn! A horse healer, for God's sake! Will she try to rub me down with liniment prescribed by some veterinarian? What was my mother thinking?

****

Inside the bathroom, Jessi placed the lantern on the floor and glanced around. The small room, probably once a pantry or large closet of some sort, had been outfitted with a shower stall, a toilet, and a wash basin with a mirror above it in the barest, most purely utilitarian manner. The fixtures looked new, even though the basin and toilet sported rings around their bowls. A clump of towels lay heaped on the floor, with a couple more stuffed onto a rack between the shower and basin.

The robe hung where he'd said it would be. She reached into her pocket and pulled out her cell. Would it work after the drenching it had gotten? She tried to reach her parents' ranch but got no response. Maybe she could make contact after the storm. She shoved it into the pocket of the robe and began to remove her soaked clothing. When she was free of it all, she took the garment from its peg and wrapped herself in its soft, navy blue terrycloth.

Relieved to be dry and comforted by the robe's luxurious texture, she paused to look into the mirror and grimaced. Not only had she come on bitter and nasty, she looked like a creature from a black lagoon. Definitely not the way to start to gain a man's confidence…or respect.

She picked up a comb lying on a small shelf under the mirror and tugged it through her bedraggled hair. Finally, deciding it was the best she could do, she gathered up her wet clothes, hung them on the peg, and sucked in a deep breath.

Okay, let's try this again.

Lantern in hand, she headed back to the kitchen.

She found him at the woodstove, stirring something that smelled delicious in a pot.

"Figured you could do with something warm," he muttered without turning to face her.

"Most definitely." She stifled the urge to go to help him as he reached into a cupboard for a bowl and staggered as he tried to balance on his good leg. "That smells wonderful."

"Seafood chowder." Turning toward her, he paused and stared.

"What?" She glanced down at her bare feet and back up at him.

"Nothing, nothing." He shoved aside Styrofoam containers to put the bowl onto the table with more vehemence than necessary. "Sit. Eat." He dropped a spoon beside it.

"Fine, Tarzan." She attempted a joke.

"What?" He scowled over at her as she took the chair he indicated.

"Oh, for God's sake, Ross, give it up. We both got off on the wrong foot, what with the storm and all. Let's declare a truce."

"Yeah, well, okay." He dropped down into the chair opposite her.

"Better. Now why don't you introduce me to your

friend?" She indicated the little red dog.

"I call her Fox. I found her on my doorstep the day I arrived. A stray, I guess."

"Hello, Fox." Jessi smiled at her. The little canine backed up against Ross's leg and sat down to stare up at the newcomer.

"Like master, like dog." She spooned into the steaming chowder and tasted. "Hmmm. Delicious. I had no idea you could cook."

"I didn't make it. A neighbor sent it over."

"Let me guess." She paused, spoon hovering over the bowl. "Dr. Shelby Masters?"

"She made it, but it was her wrangler Grady Wilson who delivered it. How did you know?"

"Your mother told me…"

"Of course. She'd have given you a crash course not only about me but my surroundings." Sarcasm laced the words.

"She was being considerate. After all, she was sending me into unfamiliar territory. She thought Dr. Masters and I might become friends."

"Aha. Two horse healers. Makes sense…that is, if you were going to be here long enough to get familiar with the neighbors."

"I don't know exactly how long you think it takes a person to become a friend to another, but I'm here for two weeks. My return ticket is dated fourteen days from now."

"Jesus."

"I can do without the cussing, thank you very much."

"I'd apologize, except that I know you've been around men and horses long enough to have heard worse."

"Ross, Ross." She shook her head and returned her attention to her chowder.

She finished her meal in silence except for the raging of the storm about the house and the sounds Ross made as he grappled to his feet and went to the refrigerator for his fourth beer.

"Don't you think you've had enough?" She jerked her head toward the three empties on the table as he screwed off the cap. "If you're taking any pain medication…"

"Ah, so now it begins." He slumped back onto his chair.

"What begins?"

"The list of do's and don't's."

"That wasn't a don't. It was simply a caution. Beer and painkillers aren't a good mix." A memory of Clint high on the combination after he'd taken a major spill flipped across her mind.

"Consider me warned. Now," he continued, "I've been sleeping in the parlor on the couch. You can take it tonight. I'll use a chair."

"Aren't there bedrooms upstairs?"

"Yeah, but falling ceiling plaster has pretty much made them unsafe."

"Okay." She resisted the impulse to tell him to take the couch and stood. "I'll head in there now." She carried her bowl and spoon to the counter and caught herself as she reached to rinse them. No electricity, no water pump.

"Good night." Picking up the lantern she'd used to find her way to the bathroom, she headed down the hallway.

"Parlor to the left," he muttered after her.

****

After he'd finished his beer, feeling a nasty little tingle of defiance as he did, the storm appeared to be lessening. At least the lightning had stopped and the old place no longer shook from thunder.

He heaved himself out of his chair and grabbed a jacket from a peg by the door. "I'm guessing she'll have confiscated my bedding, such as it is. Best be prepared. Come on, dog. Time to hit the hay…or whatever we can find to sleep on."

Taking up the remaining lantern, he followed the way she'd taken down the hall a half hour earlier, the little dog at his heels.

In the ragged Victorian parlor, he paused in the doorway to stare at her asleep on the couch. She'd left the lantern burning low on the mantel, and now she lay swathed in the soft shadows it created. She'd wrapped herself in his sleeping bag, her head pillowed on a shabby needlework cushion. With her long, golden brown hair now nearly dry and spread out over the old pillow, she gave him a start.

He'd forgotten how downright pretty Jessi Wallace was. Or maybe she'd gotten even prettier in those years he'd been so embroiled in competition he'd never taken time to notice a nice girl like her. He'd contented himself with a few one-night stands with women like Cat Holt.

As quietly as he could, he crossed the room, placed his lantern on the mantel beside hers, and extinguished it. No sense having two burning. Best to conserve what oil they had. No telling how long this outage could last.

He slumped into a shabby wing chair and spread

the jacket over his chest. It wouldn't be the first time he'd slept sitting up with a similar excuse for bedcovers.

But, he thought, as he tried to adjust himself into a position of comfort, it was the first time since the accident. Man, he was uncomfortable. Fox, curled up on the hearth rug, looked more comfortable. Well, it would only be for one night, two at most. He'd get rid of her by Thursday, tops. He closed his eyes.

What in hell...?

As a soft rumble reached him, he suppressed a grin. Nothing like snoring to kill amorous thoughts.

****

He woke as the first rays of a fine autumn morning peeked through the tattered curtains of the bay window. The storm had apparently blown itself out, leaving behind a sun-drenched day.

"Jesus." The curse was a mutter as he moved. Aches in what seemed like every bone in his body assaulted him.

Across the room Jessi moved and muttered but didn't awaken.

Looking over at her, the events of the previous evening gushed back, and he grimaced. He loved his mother, but sometimes the woman could come close to driving him around the bend...like now, sending a friend's daughter to fix up his life.

Struggling to be quiet and not wake her, he managed to heave himself out of the chair and make his way from the room and down the hall to the bathroom, Fox at his heels.

A shower. I need a shower. Just because I don't want the woman here is no reason I should disgust her with body odor.

Inside the bathroom, he snapped the light switch and was relieved to see the power had come back on. Now if he could just shower without slipping and falling. He had no desire to repeat past failures.

****

Jessi woke to the smell of coffee. For a moment she couldn't remember where she was or how she'd come to be in this ragtag room. Then, as reality returned, she closed her eyes again.

Damn!

Something warm and wet lapped at the hand she'd left hanging over the edge of the couch. Glancing down, she saw the little red dog Fox looking up her, eyes bright, white-tipped tail wagging.

"Well, good morning, Miss Fox." She found she could smile at the perky little creature. "Ready to be friends this morning? Maybe it was only the storm that made you stand-offish last night." She swung her feet to the floor and sat up. The robe gaped open, and she hastened to pull it shut and retie the belt.

"I smell coffee, Fox." She stood and stretched. "A good, strong cup is just what I need." She glanced toward the bay window flooded with sunlight. "Looks like it could be a much better day than yesterday. One can but hope. But first things first."

She felt in the robe's pocket and found her cell. Would it work after the drenching it had gotten the previous night? She picked it up and tiptoed into the bathroom. Once she'd closed the door, she punched in her home phone number. A sigh of relief slipped from her lips when it began to ring.

"Jessi?" Her mother answered immediately, her

tone a mix of anxiety and hope.

"Yes, Mom. Good morning."

"Are you okay, honey? We've been getting awful TV reports about the tail of a hurricane lashing your area." She stopped, then continued, "You are in New Brunswick, at the Turner Farm, right?"

"Yes, Mom. I made it. I couldn't call you last night. We lost service and power because of the storm." She snapped the light switch. "But the electricity is back on now and, from the sunshine coming in the parlor window, I'd say we're headed into a lovely day."

"Thank God!"

"Mom, I didn't check the time before I phoned, but I'm guessing it's shortly after 4:00 a.m. in Alberta and you don't sound as if I woke you."

"It is. I couldn't sleep, worrying about you. Now, I think, as soon as your dad and I finish up with the barn work I'll take a nap."

"Good. But first, will you do me a favor?"

"Of course, if I can."

"Will you phone Laura and tell her both Ross and I are okay? I know she'll be wondering, but I don't want to risk Ross overhearing my calling her. He's already convinced we're in some sort of deep conspiracy against him."

"Of course. Anything else?"

"No. Just take good care of my horses, Maisy in particular."

"Definitely. And, Jessi, if you think there's anything in the situation you can't handle, come right back home."

"Mom, this is Ross we're talking about. We've known him since he was a kid. He's a good man, just right now a bit confused and angry…at himself."

"Ross *is* a good man." Joan Wallace's words eased out, then became firm again. "Jessi, nevertheless, take care."

"I will. Love you. Give my best to Dad. See you soon."

"Love you, too."

She snugged the robe more securely about her waist, shoved the cell into its pocket, and left the bathroom.

****

"What are you wearing?" His words belched out as she stepped into the kitchen, a bundle under one arm.

"I would have thought you'd recognize your own shirt." The bundle still clutched close, she pivoted to give him a full view of the plaid flannel shirt buttoned up the front and hanging to just above her knees. "I found it in a closet by the front door. The robe wouldn't stay shut."

"Where do you think you're going dressed like that?" Seated at the table, coffee mug in hand, he scowled as she headed for the back door.

"Hopefully to find a clothes line. I need to dry my social worker suit and my underwear." She held up the roll of clothing she carried.

"Bloody hell!" he muttered as the door slammed behind her and he fought to dismiss the image of long, slender legs below that faded old shirt.

I have to get rid of her…fast.

"Found it." She came back inside and grinned at him. "Pants, jacket, and unmentionables now fluttering in the breeze. How about some breakfast? My turn to fix food."

At the refrigerator she pulled open the door and frowned. "Not much choice. Steak, eggs, and a whole bunch of beer. Oh, well, I'm good at fixing a cowboy breakfast. Don't look so grumpy. Food in your belly will do wonders to knock that storm cloud off your face. Thank goodness the electricity has come on. I'm not partial to working over a woodstove."

****

"Better?" She stood and began to clear the table.

"Not bad." The admission came out reluctantly.

"I'd be willing to bet you haven't eaten breakfast since you arrived here," she said, running water into the sink.

"If I admit to it, will you be including that fact in your report to my mother?"

"Stop it, Ross. Just stop it!" She rounded on him. "You have a mother who sincerely cares about you, who loves you enough to coerce me into coming across a continent to see to you!"

"Coerce?"

The moment the word had flown from her mouth, Jessi regretted it. He'd simply annoyed her so much...

"Sorry, bad word choice." She returned to the table to gather up the remainder of their breakfast dishes. "Your mother just thought it would be a good idea if I got away for a while. By the way..." She paused behind his chair and sniffed. "Do I detect the scent of some refreshing masculine soap product? Don't tell me you took a shower in honor of my presence."

Casting a cat-in-the-cream smirk over her shoulder, she sauntered back to the sink.

"Argh!"

"I thought we'd declared a truce of sorts. That

noise doesn't sound like it's in effect."

"Okay, okay."

"Better. Now"—she ran water over the dishes—"while these are soaking, I'd like to go and get my Jeep. Comfortable as this outfit is, I think I should be wearing something a tad more suitable if we have callers."

"We won't have callers." He heaved himself out of the chair and adjusted the cane in his hand. "But come on. Let's get to it."

"Dressed like this? You've got to be kidding. I don't dare bend over, and I doubt we'll get my vehicle freed from that tree without a bit of that kind of movement. I saw jeans in that same closet. Wait until I pull on a pair."

Shortly she was back, wearing his jeans rolled up at the bottoms and held in place by the belt from the bathrobe she'd worn the previous night. The shirt tail she'd tied into a knot at her middle. On her feet were the dress flats she'd worn the previous day.

"Good God!" he muttered.

"I had to improvise, given the selection." She cocked her head to one side and grinned. "I may even start a new fashion trend…like shabby chic or some such."

"Come on, let's get going." He headed for the door, Fox at his heels.

"Oh, my!" Once outside, Jessi had her first opportunity to take in her surroundings in the clear light of day.

"What?" He paused to look back at her.

"This place…it's absolutely lovely." She gazed across the wide, unmown lawn to the beach and bay beyond. A golden-sanded shore accentuated by driftwood and bright green marsh grass ended at the dark waters of Chaleur Bay glistening in the sunlight. Far out across the water a small sailboat was catching the slight breeze to move casually along its way. Above, in a clear blue sky, herring gulls swooped and cried out their crazy laughter. Behind the ramshackle house, barn and outbuildings, meadows, shorn of their crop of hay, stretched back until they were met by a verdant forest of spruce and pine.

"You cut the hay?" she asked, surprise in her tone.

"One of the locals apparently has a deal with my father to keep it mowed. Done before I got here."

"That was convenient." She drew a deep breath and smiled. "Gorgeous smell."

"Incurably cheerful, aren't you?" He headed for a red king cab 4x4, gleaming with chrome, parked near the back steps.

"I recall you once had your own happy streak." She followed and paused as he opened the rear door. "And a pretty good sense of humor."

"Yeah, well, both were removed when the doctors were cutting up my leg and hip. Come on, Fox."

The little dog leaped inside. Ross went to the driver's door, opened it, and levered himself into the seat.

"Come on, come on," he snapped when she paused. "You don't have to watch to make sure I can get into my own truck."

"Okay, okay." She strode around to the passenger side. "That chip on your shoulder has got to be log-sized."

He muttered something she guessed she was better off not understanding as he put on a pair of Foster

Grants that had been on the dash, shifted into drive, and headed the truck down the trail.

Bumping along the rutted track in his fancy truck, Jessi glanced furtively over at him. Somewhere, beneath the façade of belligerent, defiant human being, must remain fragments of the good-natured, good ol' boy Ross Turner had once been. It was her job to piece them back together.

Physically the man, except for the limp, was pretty much as she remembered…only maybe more so…the sunlight flashing through the windshield to highlight the blue-black sheen of his tangled dark curls, the faded T-shirt stretching across broad, muscular shoulders, the fit of worn jeans over his thighs…never mind those killer blue eyes now hidden behind the cool sunglasses.

She braked her thoughts to a skidding halt. *Don't get crazy, girl. Remember who he is and why you're here. The last thing you need in your life right now is another freewheeling cowboy…especially one given to dark moods.*

When they reached the turn where the pine lay blocking the road, her Jeep still nosed into it like some strange, metallic, foraging creature, Ross stopped his truck and got out. Jessi followed as he hobbled toward the tree's stump at the left of the road.

"Freshly felled," he muttered, pausing to look it over. "The wind, most likely. I knew this tree was getting dangerous. It should have been taken down weeks ago."

"You could have hired someone to do it," she suggested, tightening the bathrobe belt holding up his too-large jeans.

"Yeah, right! Admit to the locals I can't even take

care of my own property? I think not!"

"Okay, okay. Let's just get on with it." She threw up her hands.

"I'll back my vehicle into towing position. You tell me when I'm close enough to hook on."

"Fine."

She watched as he flung his cane into his truck and climbed in after it. He backed toward the barricade.

"A little more. Okay. Whoa! Perfect. Hold it." As she called out the directions, Jessi had a flashback to years earlier when she'd given similar directions to Ross as he'd been backing a horse trailer up to a corral at his parents' ranch. They'd been heading for a gymkhana and a day full of horse-based fun and games. It seemed so long ago, and with an entirely different man.

"Here, let me do that." Jessi hastened back to where he was trying to lever himself down on one knee to attach a tow rope around the thickest branches just above the butt.

"No, damn it, I will!" he snapped, then slipped on the wet road and fell.

Jessi made a move to help before stifling the impulse. She stood back as he cursed and struggled to regain control of his legs. When he got to his feet, he paused, breathing hard, leaning against the truck, his jeans mud-soaked from knees to ankles, his hands scratched and dirty.

"I'm surprised you didn't try to pull me up by the shirt, dust me off, and offer to kiss where it hurts," he growled, glowering over at her.

"No way." Jessi decided it was time tough love (or what she preferred to call acute therapy) kicked in.

"Let's get on with it."

Leaving him to struggle with the tow rope, she strode off to check on her Jeep.

She climbed in, pulled the key from her pocket, and inserted it into the ignition. The result was a low groaning sound, then nothing. She tried again. A shorter groan. The third time nothing.

Ross came to the driver's door. He put his hand on the roof above it and frowned down at her. "Let me try."

Jessi looked up at him. A sarcastic remark about men thinking they had a magic touch when it came to starting vehicles hovered. She stifled it. No need to build further animosity between them.

"Okay, sure." She got out and let him get behind the wheel.

He turned the key. This time the jeep issued something that sounded like a death rattle before it gave up the ghost.

"Major problem." He removed the key, swung out, and handed it to her. "I have CAA. I'll call for a tow truck. They'll take it back to the lot. It's an insured rental?"

"Yes." The word came out with the sigh she heaved. She hated the idea of no longer having her own vehicle, but the Jeep was useless as it was. If she wanted to go anywhere, which included leaving, she would have to depend on borrowing Ross's truck.

Ross pulled out his cell and made the call.

"Nothing to do now but get my stuff and go back to the farmhouse." She stared at the disabled vehicle.

"You make it sound as if you're headed for the Temple of Doom." A corner of his mouth twitched.

"I probably would be more welcome there." She pulled open the rear door and reached into the back for her suitcase.

Chapter Five

"I'm heading into town," he said two hours later. "I'm taking Fox with me."

He'd come into the kitchen in another pair of jeans and a T-shirt, neither of which bore evidence of recent laundering. Wearing her own jeans and shirt, she turned from where she was finishing up the breakfast dishes at the sink.

"Will you pick up some bread, milk, butter…?"

The back door slammed on her words.

She paused, then shrugged and returned to her work. Let him be rude and annoying. He couldn't dent her determination. Her thoughts went back to earlier that morning on the road to the farm.

Although it had discomforted her to watch him struggle, she'd let him do the major work of removing the pine from the road. It had taken over an hour, and by the time they'd finished a tow truck from CAA had arrived to pull the damaged Jeep back to the rental depot in Carleton.

On a positive note, she thought she caught a small sense of satisfaction in Ross's demeanor when they'd succeeded in freeing the Jeep before help arrived. Maybe a beginning? They'd returned to the farmhouse in Ross's mud-spattered truck, equally dirty themselves.

"Anyone home?" The question, in a woman's voice calling somewhere outside, startled her. A visitor? Here?

She strode through the house to the front door, pushed it open, and walked out into the sunshine to see a rider coming up from the beach. The sight of her mount made Jessi do a quick intake of breath. Charcoal gray with a silver mane and tail, it was one of the prettiest equines she'd ever seen. Her rider was leading a beautiful snow white horse, saddled and rider ready.

"Good morning." Her visitor stopped in the front yard and smiled at her. "I'm Shelby Brooks."

"Dr. Shelby Masters?" Jessi remembered Laura telling her about the vet who, together with her husband, owned a horse farm and riding instruction place nearby.

"That's my working title." She swung to the ground. "In everyday life, I'm Shelby Brooks, married to Jake Brooks. Jessi Wallace, I presume?"

Leading the horses, she walked forward, hand extended, welcoming smile lighting up a face Jessi thought entirely beautiful. Her hair, caught up in a ponytail, stuck out through the back of the baseball cap she wore. In jeans and a light blue T-shirt, the vet was one striking woman.

Glad she's married—Now where did that come from? As if I cared who lives next door to Ross or how downright beautiful she is.

"Nice to meet you, Doctor." Jessi smiled in return.

"Laura Turner called and suggested you might be missing your horses. I brought Silver along in case you have time for a little canter." She indicated the big albino. "In spite of his somewhat daunting size, I can assure you he's well trained and a pleasure to ride."

"I'd love to." Jessi reached to take the reins Shelby

held out to her, then stopped. "Do you mind waiting a minute until I put on boots and a hat?"

"Not a bit."

Jessie hurried inside. Shortly, she was back, riding boots and baseball cap in place.

"I miss my Stetson," she said pulling her hair, which she'd hastily scraped into a ponytail, through the break at the back. "But trying to carry it on the plane would have been a major nuisance. Wearing it wasn't an option unless I wanted to become the center of attention everywhere east of the Manitoba-Ontario border."

"Stetsons aren't common around here," her companion agreed. "But I admit a fondness for them. My husband has a few."

"He's from western Canada?"

"No."

The single-word reply brooked no further conversation on the subject of Stetsons.

"I really should lock up, but I don't have a key." Jessi put her curiosity regarding the monosyllabic response on hold and hesitated as she rubbed the gelding's nose. "Ross has gone to town."

"Not to be unkind"—Shelby looked around, her gaze ending on the dilapidated house—"but I don't think this place would be a prime target for home invaders."

"You're right." Jessi took the reins. "There is a new refrigerator full of beer, but that's about it." She moved to Silver's left side and stuck her foot into the stirrup.

"Thanks so much, Shelby. This is just what I need."

"We'll take a lope along the beach for a bit, then turn into the woods." The vet remounted.

"Sounds like a perfect plan." They swung their mounts about and cantered off down the beach into the sunshine and salt-tinged air. Jessi's spirits rose as they always did when she was aboard a fine horse.

Forget about one cranky former bull rider. Forget about that ruin of a farmhouse. Just enjoy this terrific ride along this beautiful stretch of beach.

When they'd gone about a half mile, Shelby reined to a halt and indicated a trail leading into the trees away from the shore.

"Nice place for a leisurely walk or trot," she said. "But too many exposed roots for a safe canter. Are you okay with that?"

"Sure." They trotted their horses into the lane, then slowed to walk them side by side.

"Mrs. Turner said you're here to help her son get over his injuries." Shelby Brooks launched the conversation.

"*Try* to help." She heaved an exasperated sigh. "I don't know if Laura Turner told you, I'm no psychologist or social worker. I deal exclusively with injured and traumatized horses. Or at least I did until now."

"Then if you don't mind my asking, why did you agree to come here, to travel across the continent for a case the likes of which you've never previously attempted?"

"Ross's family helped my family out big time a few years back, when my father got injured. I owe them."

"Aha. A debt of honor."

"You might say that."

"When Mrs. Turner first contacted me and said you'd be coming, I thought there was something romantic between you and her son. She sort of hinted at it."

"Laura wouldn't object if Ross and I got involved. You know, a pair of ranchers' kids teaming up. But I can assure you, there's nothing like that…and never will be."

"You sound a tad bitter." They were walking their horses slowly along the trail dappled with sunlight and shadows, cool and comfortable.

"I don't mind explaining." Jessi patted her horse's thick, arched neck, and he blew his thanks. "I was engaged to a saddle bronc rider. Last spring, the day of Ross's accident, I caught him with a female client of mine, and—let's just say they were doing more than holding hands."

"Miserable, isn't it?"

"You sound as if you speak from experience." Surprised, Jessi turned to face her new acquaintance.

"Sadly, yes. A few years back I caught my then-fiancé in my house in the arms of a naked soap opera star who spent a lot of time at her father's place just beyond my farm."

"Oh, Shelby, I'm sorry. What did you do?"

"It was winter, the first serious snowfall of the year, in fact. I threw her out, stark naked, and invited him to follow. When I discovered they'd been so bold as to make love in my bed, I burned it." She chuckled. "I can see the humor in it now, but back then it stung like getting a tree branch across the face on a frosty morning. And"—she drew a deep breath—"it turned out all for the best. That Christmas I married Jake. Maybe that's how it will be with you. Are you absolutely sure there's nothing between you and Ross Turner?"

"Nothing. We sort of grew up together, even though Ross is a few years older and lived a bunch of miles away. Anyhow, he's so belligerent right now, I'm sure romance is the furthest thing from his mind. His injury is dominating everything."

"That's what it was like with Jake after he was involved in a car accident." The trail had emerged into a meadow, and Shelby halted to look over at her companion. "He got all tied up in knots and was ready to go back to work in Toronto."

"But he didn't. Why not?"

"Because I asked him to marry me." She grinned. "I can tell you, that took the wind out his sails."

"I take it he agreed."

"After a bit of a pause and his parents' blessing, yes."

"Well, that's one cure I won't be trying." Jessi followed Shelby as she turned her mount back down the trail.

"Careful, Jessi. I thought the same way, once upon a time."

****

Looking after Ross Turner was turning out to be as much a housekeeping job as a caregiving position. Jessi gazed around the dirty, cluttered kitchen and sighed. She'd enjoyed the ride with Shelby, but now she had to face the reality of her situation and get down to work.

She hadn't had an opportunity to explore the upper story of the house. Maybe, in spite of Ross's dire warnings about falling plaster, she could make a couple of bedrooms sufficiently safe and decent for them to use. That old couch in the parlor had more lumps and bumps than a stretch of bad road, and Ross couldn't have enjoyed sleeping in that chair.

She went into the front foyer and gazed up the staircase that even on this sunny day was dark and shadowy. Threadbare carpeting ran up the center of dusty steps to a curve near the top. It looked like part of one of the haunted houses she'd seen in horror movies. What lay beyond that twist at the top?

Come on, Jessi Wallace. You've spent nights out on the range listening to coyotes howl. This is just an old farmhouse...dilapidated and dirty, nothing more.

Squaring her shoulders, she headed up the steps, rounded the turn near the stairway's zenith, and was confronted with a long, dark corridor with several closed doors along its length.

Bats. This is the point in a movie where a herd—or is it a flock?—of bats flutter out into a person's face.

None did. With a feeling of relief, she started down the hallway. She opened one door after another, to find bedrooms in such a state of neglect she abandoned any hope of their sleeping up there. The beds had been stripped of sheets, blankets, and pillows. All that was left were ragged mattresses that looked as if any number of mice had taken up residence. Shreds of sun-rotted curtains hung at the windows. Each room had an old dresser and a washstand with pitcher and ewer, a chamberpot tucked underneath giving testament that there'd been no indoor bathroom before Ross's arrival. Furthermore, true to Ross's description, chunks of fallen ceiling plaster were scattered at indiscriminate intervals, some little more than dust, others big enough to cause a concussion.

No, definitely no hope of human habitation up here. Why did I allow myself to be talked into coming to this miserable old house?

Her cell rang.

"Jessi, it's Laura. Is Ross there?"

"He went into Carleton." She started back downstairs.

"Good. It's you I want to talk to…alone. How is he doing? Jessi, I'm counting on your usual honesty."

"He's still using his cane." She paused, trying to decide how best to proceed.

"But mentally, emotionally?"

"A little grumpy, careless about his appearance." She tried to tell the truth without being alarming. "Nothing I can't handle."

"I know you can." Laura Turner sounded relieved. "But tell me he hasn't let himself go so badly he's a complete mess. I wouldn't want to think he's made himself absolutely unattractive."

"Laura, stop it. After Clint Harrison, the handsomest, most charismatic cowboy in the world wouldn't interest me."

"You're fortunate to be rid of that creature." The woman's tone turned crisp and brooked no denial. "Just like Ross is much better off without Catherine…Cat Holt. If that woman shows up anywhere near him, I'm personally deputizing you to get rid of her any way you see fit. She's pure poison."

"That's a big order."

"Okay, okay. But don't write Ross off just yet. He's a good man."

64

"Laura, nothing is going to happen between your son and me. I'm strictly here in the capacity of observer and caregiver…if he'll allow me to become the latter."

"Very well. I'll leave it for the moment. Now, tell me about your living conditions. Ross wouldn't elaborate."

"Well…" Jessi let her gaze roam around the shabby old house and decided to tell the truth.

Chapter Six

Damn it, damn it, damn it!

Ross adjusted his aching left leg and let the irritation of his mother's sending Jessi Wallace to look after him surface full force as he drove toward Carleton. He knew she meant well, was concerned about him, but sending Jessi Wallace, who worked with traumatized horses? Hell and damnation!

Top it off with the fact that he'd been celibate since over a month before his accident… Not by any major plan but simply because he'd been too involved in training and practice rides to have time to hook up with a lady. Well, if he was being totally honest, there was more to it. In spite of the reputation a lot of rodeo cowboys had for love 'em and leave 'em, he didn't fall easily into bed with one woman after another. Over the years he'd learned pure animal sex wasn't for him. He needed more than that. He wanted to like any woman he paired up with, genuinely like her.

Given that fact, it wasn't surprising none of his romances on the rodeo circuit had lasted long. Women who followed the shows and were willing to take a chance on a performer through a one-night stand weren't the type that attracted him. Women like Cat Holt. Furthermore, he wasn't about to buy a ring or make any kind of long-term commitment to anyone…not yet, maybe never. He'd never met a woman who gave him the urge to do either.

His thoughts went back to Jessi Wallace. A really nice girl who knew her way around animals, horses in particular. And pretty as the proverbial picture, with her golden-brown hair and green eyes that seemed to be able to peer right down into his thoughts.

Watch it, buddy. Don't start having crazy fantasies about her.

It was bad enough his mother had sent her to doctor him like a lame horse, but now she was living under his roof, sleeping in the same room. He'd have to keep himself on a short rein. If he messed up with her, he had no doubt he'd find Laura Turner on his doorstep with a shotgun in one hand and a bridal veil in the other.

A grin quirked one corner of his mouth.

Yeah, Mom, you'd love to get me married off to Jessi Wallace, wouldn't you? Someone to settle me down, get me to start helping Chase around the place. Well, put that thought on hold. It won't be happening. Right now I have to concentrate on getting my would-be caregiver on a flight back to Calgary.

He knew there'd be no way a lady as strong and stubborn as Jess would simply acquiesce to going home. He sucked in a deep breath and centered his mind on how to go about it.

First, a trip to the barber. Then a bit of grocery shopping, followed by a visit to a florist and the liquor store. Mom always said you could get more flies with honey than vinegar. Hope that doctor didn't remove any ability I once had to charm a lady, when he operated on my leg. I'll need every bit I can muster, if I'm going to finesse Miss Jessi Wallace.

He glanced at Fox sitting alertly in the passenger seat. *Wonder if there's a dog groomer in Carleton? My little gal could do with a bit of sprucing up, too.*

****

"I bought groceries…" Ross's voice trailed off as he entered the kitchen, a plastic bag in his free hand, and stopped dead in his tracks. Fox darted inside ahead of his master.

Jessi turned from wiping down a countertop. And froze.

Clean-shaven and with a spanking new haircut, Ross the Uncouth had been transformed into Ross the Rodeo Rock Star. His T-shirt and jeans looked brand new, his boots polished.

"Well." She finally found her voice. "It seems we've both been busy."

"Yeah, really." Leaning on his cane, he gazed over clean sinks, cleared countertops, and freshly swept floor.

"I hope I haven't ruined the ambience." She couldn't resist the taunt. Two large bags of garbage leaned against the wall near the door.

"Ambience? What ambience? Early Canadian landfill?"

"Gave me something to do…after I went riding with your neighbor, Dr. Shelby Masters-Brooks."

"Riding?" He dropped the grocery bag he'd been carrying onto the table and stared at her.

"She rode over from her farm. She brought a lovely white gelding all tacked up for me. We had a great canter up the beach, then a lovely walk through the woods. Shelby's quite a lady. We had a nice chat."

"Oh, yeah?"

"Take that note of suspicion out of your voice. I didn't reveal any of your deep, dark secrets…not that I know any. Hey…" She turned her attention to Fox. "Looks as if you had a makeover as well, little girl. You're positively gleaming…golden red, I'd call your new look." She knelt to hug the dog that sat in front of her, tail swishing over the floor.

"Yeah, well, there was a grooming place right next to the barber shop, so…"

"Well, she looks great." Jessi stood and indicated the meat on a plate on the counter. "I defrosted a couple of the steaks for supper. Not a great deal of choice. Really, Ross, your larder is in bad shape."

"I know."

He turned and hobbled out to his truck. Jessi took the opportunity to grab a glass of cold water. The man, freed from all that hair and neglect, was a knockout, definitely something that would warm any woman's blood…even hers.

"Will you get the door?" His voice brought her out of her daydreams, and she hurried over to open it. He came in, his free arm full of more plastic grocery bags.

"I've let my supplies dwindle," he said, placing the bags on the kitchen table. "So I decided to stock up."

"Do you need any help?" The words were out before she could catch her normal reaction.

"No, no." He waved aside her offer and headed back outside.

****

Bread, milk, eggs, butter, and so much more…so much unexpected more. Jessi, unloading the grocery bags, found fresh vegetables, rolls, cheese, several bottles of salad dressing, and a sumptuous-looking carrot cake, individually packaged. The final bag contained a selection of gourmet dog food.

What is going on?

Jessi was putting lettuce into the refrigerator when she heard his cane stump up the back steps again, then stop. Turning, she saw him standing in the doorway, a bouquet of red roses in his hand, a bottle of wine clutched under his arm. Fox stood beside him, bright and perky, tail wagging.

Oh, God, why did he have to clean up so well? And why does he have to look so romance-novel-cover handsome standing there with those roses and that adorable dog? And that grin...and those blue eyes.

"I've come a-callin', Miss Jessi, ma'am." He grinned.

"Really?" Warning bells were all-out clanging in her brain. *What is he up to? Watch it, Jessi Wallace, watch it.*

She cocked her head to one side. "I hope your intentions are honorable, young man, and not part of a plot to get rid of me."

"Only the purest, I assure you, missy," he replied, awkwardly levering the door open. "You see, I'm under sentence of having my favorite horse sold by my own dear mama if I stepped even the least out of line with you." His voice softened seductively as he eased the dozen long stems into her arms. "For you, lady," he said.

Blue gaze met green and held. A sensation like stepping into a tub full of perfectly warm bath water slid over her.

"Thank you." *No, no, no, not another rodeo cowboy!* She caught herself up short. "I'll put these in water."

She headed for the sink. "Red roses are my favorite."

"My mother may have mentioned it." He swung himself about on his cane and went back outside.

Running water into a vase, she dampened her fingers and patted the cool wetness to her hot cheeks. She'd heard of magic moments, but this was ridiculous.

****

"Steaks are ready." Ross opened the front door and stuck his head inside. He'd insisted on cooking them over the coals of a fire he'd built in a pit in front of the house.

"Terrific. I'm starving." Jessi picked up a large bowlful of salad and joined him on the front porch, where she'd found an old wooden table just big enough for two people to share a meal.

As she placed the salad on the table, she saw he'd opened the wine and put the bottle in the center. Foil-wrapped potatoes he'd roasted in the fire pit were in a bowl beside it.

"Medium rare?" He hobbled up the verandah steps, two T-bones on a platter in his free hand. Fox, sniffing appreciatively, followed at his heels.

"Right. Those look delicious."

"I agree." He placed the food on the table, then swung himself around to pull out a weathered chair for her. "Let's hope neither of us breaks through these elegant seats."

As she accepted his offer, he flashed a smile in her direction that gave her goose bumps. The man was totally gorgeous, there was no use denying it, and he could be absolutely charming when he wanted to be.

But a small suspicious voice in her mind kept asking, *Why now? Why this sudden turnaround?*

"Wine?" He held the bottle over her glass.

"Please." She decided to dismiss her suspicions with the fact that she was capable of looking after herself no matter what his motives were for this display of gentlemanly charm.

"Jess, we haven't really talked about this arrangement my mother foisted on us," he said once he'd poured a measure into both their glasses and taken a chair opposite her. "We've been too busy sniping at each other about a situation neither of us is responsible for. When I had time to think today on the drive to Carleton, I came to the conclusion we have to take stock of our circumstances coolly and calmly and decide how best to deal with them."

She narrowed her eyes as she looked over at him. "Okay, I'm listening."

"I know I've been anything but cooperative, or even civil," he continued. "I'm ready to concede the fact. I'm also sure you didn't want to come here any more than I wanted a nursemaid. Purely out of love and concern, my mother manipulated us both. Therefore, purely out of our love and concern for her, we might at least try to put her mind at ease by appearing to go along with her plans…at least for a little while."

He looked over at her, blue eyes far too appealing for Jessi's comfort.

Remember Clint Harrison. He has blue eyes, too.

"Sure, why not? Anything for Laura," she replied hoping she sounded offhanded.

"Good." He moved forward in his chair, picked up the bowl of potatoes, and offered it to her. "But," he continued as she took one, "in actual fact, I won't be spoon-fed or ordered around. I will continue to do exactly as I please. Understood?"

"But I thought you said you were willing to go along with your mother's wishes." Her hand stopped in midair as she met a gaze that had suddenly gone steel cold with determination.

"I said 'by appearing to go along with her plans,' " he said, taking the bowl out of her hand. He dropped a pair of potatoes onto his plate, replaced the container at center table, and picked up his wineglass. "Understood?"

She hesitated.

"Understood," she said finally, slowly. Then, picking up the other plate, she offered it to him. "Roll?" she asked with an innocently seductive gleam in her eyes.

****

She was putting plates into the sink when she became aware of his presence close behind her.

"Yes?" she asked, turning to face him.

"That was a nice meal."

"I enjoyed it. Glad you saw fit to buy the trimmings."

"Jess…" He looked down at his boots. "I've had a devil of a time to keep from becoming totally antisocial since this leg thing. I apologize."

"Apology accepted. You're going through a rough patch. I understand."

"Then we're good?"

"We're good." She turned back to the sink and began to run water into it.

"Leave those." He put a hand on her arm, and she

turned to see something too warm and suggestive for comfort in his eyes. "Come out on the veranda and have another glass of wine. It's a great evening…bit of a moon rising over a bay that's smooth as glass. We shouldn't waste it. It might be just what Dr. Laura would order at this point for both of us."

"You think so?" His suggestion conjured up the memory of Laura Turner daring Jessi to resist her handsome son on a romantic evening alone with him. Now here stood Ross Turner, all six foot two of him, broad-shouldered and handsome beyond the legal limit, offering her a moment of magic in the warm September night.

She *did* have a pretty fail-safe firewall, she reminded herself. Clint's betrayal was still fresh in her mind.

"Fine." She turned off the water. "Let's go."

****

Later, seated beside him on an old porch swing at the far end of the veranda, Jessi Wallace was having second thoughts. A gorgeous sunset over the bay had metamorphosed into the dark velvet of a soft autumn night punctuated with stars and a curl of a new moon. A breeze, gentle and hinting of the sea, wafted in off the water. And beside her was a man who could be Mr. September on any Chippendale calendar.

Handsome, sexy, and incredibly virile Ross Turner sat next to her in the dark lace of softly swaying tree shadows and told the story of a small island about a quarter mile off shore in front of the farm.

"According to family legend, all kinds of marine outlaws are reputed to have used it as a hideout," he explained, leaning back beside her. "There's a deep, narrow channel between it and this shore."

"Were there any stories of treasure buried out there?"

"Not that I've ever heard. If there'd been any hint of such a possibility, the place probably would have been excavated to the core."

"Hmmm." An idea brightened in Jessi's mind. "I'd still like to visit the place. Is there a boat around here?"

"There's an old skiff down near the shore. I doubt it's seaworthy."

"What say we give it a try?"

"I'll take the idea under consideration." He reached for the bottle on the table in front of them. "More wine? Normally, as you know, I'm a beer drinker, but this stuff isn't half bad."

"Why not?"

When their glasses had been replenished, he pulled his phone from his pocket, scrolled through it for a moment, then tapped. *Moon River* wafted out into the warm, moonlit night. With an effort he tried to disguise, he got to his feet.

"Dance?"

"What?" Astounded by the offer, Jessi stared up at him.

"Dance. With you to support me, I think I might be able to handle this old tune."

"Ross, what are you up to?" She narrowed her eyes as she looked up at him.

"Nothing, nothing. The desire to try just came to me. But if you don't want to…"

"No, no, of course not." She stood. *Can't discourage any bit of initiative he's willing to try.*

He laid his cane up against the veranda railing and

took her into his arms. For a moment, he hesitated, looking up at her through the soft black veil of summer night shadows. A butterfly feeling fluttered inside her.

"It's been a long time," he muttered, and Jessi didn't know if he meant since he'd danced or since he'd held a woman in his arms.

"All the more reason to get back in the game." She struggled to sound casual.

"Okay, let's give this a go."

As he drew her against his body and his hand found the small of her back, she caught the scent of his aftershave and was struck by a myriad of sensations so powerful they knocked her physically and emotionally off balance. When he started to move slowly, almost cautiously, in time to the music, she stumbled.

"Sorry," he said softly, his lips close to her ear. "I warned you."

"My fault," she managed, but the words sounded falsetto and shaky. She tried for a recovery. "You're doing just fine."

"Am I?" He drew her out from him enough to look down into her face. "Am I, Jessi Wallace?" The words thickened with sensuous double meaning. Slowly, very slowly he lowered his head to kiss her.

Ross, Ross, Ross. His name gushed over her in a wild, impetuous wave, pulling her under, drowning her in the moment. She hadn't been expecting this or anything like it. Her feet seemed to leave the warped planking of the old veranda floor. Her senses grew wings and soared.

Then he was letting her surface, raising his head to study her expression in the moonlight.

"You're beautiful," he said softly. "And you

smell"—he nuzzled her neck, her ear—"like an evening breeze after a summer shower."

"Ross..." His name was a prolonged exhale. "Please..."

"Please what, Jess? Stop? Keep going? What do you want me to do? I'm all yours. Totally seduced."

"Seduced?" The spell snapped, and she yanked herself out of his arms. "This dance was supposed to be therapy, a chance to see what you can do!"

"Right." He grinned down at her.

"Oh, Ross, stop it!" She slapped his chest with the flat of her hand. "Don't go giving double meanings to a purely innocent..."

"Sure, sure." He caught her by the shoulders, planted a final quick kiss on her lips, then grinning turned, picked up his cane, and hobbled into the house. "See you in the morning, Nurse."

Left alone on the verandah, Jessi crossed her arms tightly across her chest. Her eyes narrowed in anger. She willed her heart, or something in her chest, to stop beating a tattoo.

Okay, score one for the cowboy, but Jessi Wallace wasn't about to concede the game.

Chapter Seven

He feigned sleep in the chair in the parlor when she entered the room, but through a slit below one eyelid he saw she'd changed into flannel pajamas decorated with galloping horses.

Thank God for small blessings! He'd had a hard enough time dragging himself in off the veranda after that hot kiss. If she'd showed up wearing anything even vaguely sexy...

"Good night, cowboy." She dropped down onto the couch and gathered his sleeping bag around herself. "I know you're faking."

He suppressed a mutter as he pulled his jacket over his chest and tried to get comfortable.

What in hell is she referring to...faking sleep? Or that kiss?

There'd been one good result of that encounter, he thought as a smug smile pulled at his mouth. The lack of response with Cat hadn't been his fault. That kiss with Jessi had proven he could get back in the game any time he chose.

****

He woke, sweating, his leg aching like fire. A cramp in his right shoulder didn't help the situation.

Hell and damnation, this is one miserable place to sleep. The woman could at least have offered to take turns on the couch.

He tried to resettle himself to sleep by reminding himself he'd always been his own man and he wasn't about to change now. No way was he getting involved with that woman sleeping across the room, honey-colored hair spread out over a ratty old pillow, curvy body stretched in his sleeping bag.

Feeling chafed to the bone, he wondered if she would've had the courage to return that kiss so boldly if she hadn't been confident in Laura Turner's assurance she'd warned her son to be a gentleman at all times. His mother wouldn't have told Jessi that one of her reasons for sending her to New Brunswick was in the hope they would form a relationship that would convince him to marry and settle down to ranching. Or would she?

The Jessi Wallace he knew would never commit to such a scheme. No, he was sure Jessi was as much a pawn in his mother's game of hearts as he was, probably even more so, since she didn't know Laura Turner as well as he did and probably didn't suspect her ulterior motive in sending her down to care for him.

Grudgingly he had to admit the woman had made a good choice. If he, Ross Turner, was going to consider settling down and getting married, Jessi Wallace might be a candidate. They shared similar backgrounds, both loved the western lifestyle, and both were good at living it.

Remembering her arrival on his doorstep, he let a grin quirk his lips. Even dripping wet, she was beautiful. In fact, the way her clothes had clung to every curve of her body had made him all too conscious of just how long it had been since he'd enjoyed intimate female companionship.

He forced it down. He had to. This time his mother

had definitely brought in the heavy artillery. Well, he wasn't about to fall victim to his mother's plots or plans, no matter how well intentioned. He, Ross Turner, had already set up a no-fail counterattack.

Clutching his jacket/blanket he stood, suppressing a grunt of discomfort. With Fox at his heels, he headed for the front porch and the swing at one end. He'd always enjoyed sleeping outdoors. The farther he got away from her, the sooner he'd be able to relax and settle down to some serious rest. And tomorrow he'd be back in scheming mode.

****

"Good morning." He smiled at her as she came into the kitchen. "Looks like it's going to be a warm one. I see you've dressed for it." He glanced at her tan walking shorts and yellow tank top. *Damn it, she's got great legs.*

She shot him a withering glance as she strode past him to the percolator.

"Look, I'm sorry about last night." He limped over to stand beside her as she took a mug from a cupboard and poured coffee into it. "What I did was in self defense. I was checking your motives for coming down here…seeing if they were as altruistic as they were supposed to be."

Liar. The word echoed in his mind as he offered the explanation. He'd been intrigued, attracted…on a purely physical level, of course.

"I'm that suspicious and intimidating, am I?" She looked up at him, green eyes as cold as emeralds in a snowstorm.

"Suspicious? No, I don't think so…not anymore." He turned to rest his hips against the counter and face her squarely, arms crossed on his broad, white T-shirted chest, and favored her with what he hoped was a disarming grin. "Intimidating? Yeah, I guess you could be considered intimidating. So from now on, no more slow dancing in the moonlight, no matter how therapeutic, okay?"

"Okay, fine." She went to the refrigerator. "Bacon, eggs," she went over the inventory. "I'll fry them up, and you can make toast and brew fresh coffee." She grimaced down into her cup. "You must have made this stuff at dawn and measured it with a forklift."

"Yeah, well, you are right about that first part." He couldn't tell her the thoughts of her had kept him awake. "Fox woke me at dawn, and I couldn't get back to sleep."

"Okay." She gave him a long look that reminded him of a teacher he'd had in the third grade who could always tell when he was lying. "Did you go out somewhere last night? I woke about three and you weren't in the chair."

"Found it more comfortable in the porch swing. Did you think I'd snuck out for a booty call?"

"You're free to do as you please." She shrugged, and she *almost* sounded indifferent. *Or is that wishful thinking?*

"I was thinking," he hastened on as she took a frying pan from a hook above the stove and brought it down on one of the burners with more vehemence than necessary. "My mother wants me to see a doctor in Moncton. Some sort of sports injury expert."

"Yes?" She laid rashers of bacon side by side in the pan.

God, can't the woman speak without making me

feel like squirming?

"Well, what say we take a drive down there today?"

"What!" She swung to face him, astonishment registered in her expression. "Laura said you're determined never to see another doctor."

"Can't a man change his mind?" The words came out with a tone of annoyance he hadn't intended. Lying definitely wasn't his thing.

"Sure, of course." She returned her attention to the meat in the pan. "Just that guys as stubborn as bull riders usually take a lot more persuading."

"Okay, okay. So I'm thinking if I go, it might just be a way to get you and her off my back…for a while."

"Fine." She watched the bacon begin to curl in the hot pan. "We'll leave as soon as we've eaten." Then she turned on him. "But don't you have to have an appointment? Specialists seldom if ever take off-the-street patients."

"My mother made it weeks ago. I'd planned to cancel at the last minute…put me in the black books with a high-end doctor who has patients waiting for months to see him."

"Aha. I might have guessed." She went to the refrigerator for eggs. "Okay, I'll change after breakfast, and we'll hit the road."

Good. Everything going according to plan.

****

They left for Moncton an hour later, in Ross's truck, with him driving. Jessi had expected the three-hour journey to be silent and tense. Instead, Ross drew her into conversation about rodeos they'd both attended, horses they were both familiar with, and their lives as kids growing up on successful ranches. By the time they reached the city, both were laughing over shared memories. When Ross suggested lunch at a seafood restaurant, she agreed without hesitation.

"The lobster rolls are great here," he said as the waiter gathered up their menus and turned away. "I stopped in for a meal when I arrived at the airport a few weeks ago, while I was waiting to pick up my rental truck. I also saw something you might enjoy. You can watch it in about"—he looked at his watch—"a half hour. It's called the Tidal Bore, when the tidal waters of the Bay of Fundy rush in against the Petitcodiac River's current to create a wave surfers can ride for miles. Worth a view."

"Sounds like a plan."

Jessi settle back in the comfortable chair and relaxed. She would have been enjoying the day completely if a nagging little voice in the back of her mind hadn't kept asking why Ross the Difficult had suddenly become Prince Charming.

****

"Damn it!"

As they were leaving the restaurant, Ross's cane caught in a crack in the steps leading down to the sidewalk. He toppled against Jessi, catching at the strap of her shoulder bag in a last-ditch effort to save himself. His weight wrenched it from her arm and sent it skittering.

"Hell!" he exploded, righting himself against her shoulder, then shrugged away as she tried to steady him. "Rotten, stupid…"

"Ross, there are kids behind us!"

"Okay, okay."

"My purse." Jessi turned to look for it, but he was already hobbling toward where it lay against a step front. She followed. As she caught up to him, he bent to pick it up and his hand grasped its strap, but he lost his balance. In his efforts to right himself, he bumped the clasp, which released and let the purse's contents spew across the sidewalk.

"Argh!" Something like an animal snarl erupted from him.

"It's okay." Jessi moved to help as he dropped with a grunt onto his good knee and began to gather up lipstick, wallet, keys, and the rest of her belongings.

"No, damn it, I made the mess, I'll clean it up." His words brooked no refusal, and she backed off.

"Sorry. I didn't mean to bark at you." His tone softened. "You go on to the waterfront. There's a lookout right over there." He pointed to the left. "The Tidal Bore is due any minute. I don't want you to miss it. I'll gather up your stuff and meet you there."

"Well…"

"Go, go!" He waved her away. "Go now, or you'll miss it."

She hesitated only a second longer before hurrying away.

Jessi joined the group of spectators as the world's highest tides from the Bay of Fundy rushed in against the current of the Petitcodiac River to create a wave of backlash. Several surfers were actually riding it.

"Amazing, isn't it?"

Entranced by the spectacle, Jessi hadn't noticed Ross joining her, purse in his hand.

"Wonderful," she agreed, smiling up at him. "I'm glad you gave me the opportunity to see it. Thanks for staying behind to pick up my stuff."

She was about to open the bag to check its contents when he caught her by the arm. "Time to go. My doctor's appointment is in ten minutes. I'll drop you at the mall next door to his office. You can spend the wait time shopping. I'll meet you in the coffee shop of the hotel two doors down from the mall at four p.m., okay? If I'm going to be delayed longer, I'll leave a message for you at the front desk."

****

Jessi glanced at her watch as she sat in the coffee shop. Three forty-five. Deciding she had time for a latté, she ordered one. As the waiter placed it in front of her, she opened her purse to get her wallet.

Where is it?

Placing the bag on the counter, she began what was at first a routine search, then turned into a downright doggy-dig to its bottom. She hadn't made any purchases at the mall, so she knew she couldn't have left it there. Finally she had to admit the truth. The wallet that held her credit cards, cash, and ID was missing.

"Is something wrong?" the young man waiting to be paid asked.

"Yes…no…that is, my wallet with all my cash and credit cards is missing."

"Did you leave your purse unattended? Robberies can happen pretty darned fast."

"No."

"Do you want me to notify the police?"

Jessi saw a folder tucked into a side pocket. It hadn't been there previously. Gingerly she took it out and examined the contents. Inside was a shuttle pass from the hotel to the Moncton Airport and a one-way first-class ticket on a red-eye that evening to Calgary.

"No, thank you, that won't be necessary." She narrowed her eyes. "I know who the perpetrator is, and the law can't possibly punish him enough!"

****

"I have a one-way, first-class Air Canada ticket to Calgary...cheap." Jessi fluttered the envelope under the nose of the startled desk clerk in the hotel's main lobby and tried to contain the fury engulfing her. "Fifty dollars will buy it. I'm in a huge hurry. I have to catch the bus to Carleton, and it's leaving in fifteen minutes!"

She was seething with volcanic intensity when a pleasant-looking man in his thirties wearing a courier's uniform approached her.

"Did I hear you say you had a one-way airline ticket to Calgary for sale for fifty dollars?" he asked. "Is it non-refundable?"

She nodded. "For a nine-thirty flight this evening. Do you know of someone who'll buy it?"

"Well, I can't actually pay you," he said slowly. "But maybe we can make a deal." He took her arm and drew her away from the desk, beyond the hearing of the clerk. "I take it you want to get to Carleton?"

She nodded vehemently. "In the worst way. There's...something I have to do." She avoided telling him it was premeditated murder.

"How about this for an idea?" He leaned closer. "I'll give you a drive to Carleton right now in exchange for that ticket. I have a delivery up there. I'm not supposed to take passengers, but I'm darned near as desperate as you look. My wife's brother's been freeloading off us for a month, but he keeps claiming all he really wants is a ticket out west to get a job. Well, thanks to you, he might just get his wish…one way. What do you say?"

"Just a minute," she said and went back to speak to the desk clerk.

"Do you know that man?" she asked softly.

"Danny?" He looked past her at the uniformed driver. "Sure. A great guy. Wife and three kids. A real family man. He's been driving for the same company for over ten years."

"Thanks." She returned to the man.

"You've got a deal," she told him as a roll of thunder, announcing an approaching storm, echoed through the hotel.

"Give me a minute." An expression of relieved pleasure enveloping his face, he took the ticket and pulled out his cell. "I'm going to tell my lay-around brother-in-law to start packing. He can pick up the ticket here at the hotel desk. By this time tomorrow he'll be thousands of miles away."

Chapter Eight

"Ross Turner?" The driver of the delivery truck peered in through the screen door, clipboard in hand. Ross had barely gotten back inside the house after his trip to Moncton when the man arrived. He'd been about to let Fox out for a run after her hours of confinement, but hearing a vehicle churning down the lane toward the farm, he'd decided to keep her inside until he saw who and what it was.

"Yeah." Ross looked out at the vehicle parked a few feet from his rear porch. "Why?"

"Delivery for you." He started back down the steps. "Better keep the little dog out of the way while Harry backs up."

"What in hell?" Ross stood staring as the burly man returned to the truck and began to wave his arms in directing the driver to back up toward the porch. As he realized the wisdom in the delivery man's words, he slammed the screen door shut in time to keep Fox inside.

A couple of hours later, he stood staring at the results of the delivery.

Two mattresses and box springs lay on the parlor floor, with a stack of sheets, pillows, and blankets piled on top. In the kitchen, a washer and dryer had been swiftly installed, as well as a four-burner, full-sized electric stove. Before the delivery man left, he'd handed

Ross an envelope. Inside was a note that read, "A few things I thought you might need. Love, Mom."

Damn it, what did Jessi tell you? Laura Turner, you'll never cease to amaze me...even while you're busy driving me nuts. God, what a day! I need a beer.

He strode into the kitchen and pulled open the refrigerator.

"Damn it!" He stared inside at the two remaining bottles. "Cupboard's almost bare." He looked down at the little dog looking eagerly up at him. "Guess we'll have to make a run to Carleton." He glanced at her freshly emptied bowl. "Had enough to satisfy you?" He'd fed her as soon as the delivery men left. "Want to come along? You had a long day alone here in the house."

In answer, Fox ran to the door and barked, tail wagging.

"Okay, let's go."

As he let the dog jump into the passenger seat, he stopped himself from further conversation with her. Time to stop talking to a dog and get on with his life.

But as he turned the truck down the lane, he passed the spot where pieces of pine branches marked the place where the big tree had blocked the road, and an image of Jessi Wallace crashed across his mind with the force of a mental tsunami. When had she become such a downright beautiful woman? Had he been on the circuit so long he hadn't had a chance to notice?

Why the hell should I care?

He eased his vehicle over the remaining branches and on down the road.

She's gone. I got rid of her once and for all. When she arrives back in Alberta, my mother will realize she'll have to get up a lot earlier in the morning to outsmart her boy.

In Carleton, he pulled into the liquor store parking lot and got out.

"Cute dog," a lady passing smiled, looking at Fox in the truck window. "Yours?"

"Thanks. She was a stray."

"What a shame. She appears to be a purebred Little River Duck Dog."

"A what?"

"A Little River Duck Dog. The breed originated in Yarmouth, Nova Scotia. I lived there a few years ago and got acquainted with them. Absolutely lovely creatures, so clever and sensitive. Are you going to keep her?"

"Yeah, sure, I guess."

"Oh, how lovely! I'm always happy to hear about a dog getting a good home."

He continued on into the store. When he returned, carrying the largest box of beer the store had to offer, he saw a pair of scruffy-looking men peering into the truck on the driver's side. Fox was pressed against the opposite door, teeth bared.

"Something I can do for you?" Ross hefted the beer into the cargo space and turned to them.

"The dog." One of them dared to confront Ross. "I heard you tellin' that woman she's a stray. Well, she's mine."

"Yeah?" Ross glanced in at Fox's snarling reaction before turning back to the man. "She doesn't seem to like you much."

"Yeah, well, she can be the right little bitch. I'll let you have her for fifty bucks, no questions asked."

"Will you, now?" Ross crossed his arms and drew himself up. The man backed off a couple of steps but repeated, "Fifty bucks and she's all yours."

"Okay, well, maybe before I decide whether or not to pay up, we should check out your claim." Ross reached for the handle and started to open the door. "Call her by name."

"Hell, don't do that!" The man and his friend were backing away as Fox advanced across the seat, snarling. "You can keep the damned thing!"

Grinning at their retreating figures, Ross opened the door to get in. Before he could stop her, Fox bolted past him and off in pursuit of the two men who, seeing her coming, broke into a run, heading around behind the liquor store.

"Fox!" Ross slammed the truck door and strode after her. "Fox!"

An hour later, Ross Turner stood outside the bulletproof glass of the reception area of the Carleton Detachment of the RCMP and reported a missing dog.

"I'm sorry, sir," The officer on duty told him. "We don't deal with lost pets. You should file a report with the SPCA."

"I already did, but there were these two guys who tried to blackmail me out of fifty bucks in the liquor store parking lot, claiming to be her rightful owners. She took off after them, and I'm thinking they might have caught her..."

"Blackmailers in the liquor store parking lot?" Ross saw skepticism registered in the officer's expression and had to struggle to contain his annoyance.

"Look, I wasn't drinking then and I'm not drinking

now. You can step out here and smell my breath or breathalyze me or whatever you want to do. If you can't take a complaint of a missing dog"—he refused to use the term pet—"I'll make a report of stolen property. How's that?"

The officer looked at him for a moment, then heaved a deep breath. "Sorry, sir, there's nothing more…"

"What seems to be the problem, Constable?" A tall, dark-haired man entered and strode to join Ross in front of the desk. Above a pair of jeans, he was wearing a navy sweatshirt with an image of a grinning Pug dog emblazoned across its front. A caption read "Bruiser."

"This gentleman has lost his dog, Sergeant." *Sergeant, in that getup?* "I'm trying to explain we don't take lost dog reports, that he should deal with the SPCA."

"Let me handle this." The man, who appeared to be in great shape and not exactly ugly, indicated chairs in the waiting area. "Have a seat, Mr.…"

"Turner, Ross Turner. I'm staying out at the old Turner farm on the shore road."

"Ah, yes. We heard someone new had moved in there. Bull rider from Alberta, right?"

"Right, but how…?"

"We make it our business to investigate new residents who move into remote places and aren't obviously family people."

"Aha. Drugs. I get it."

"Possibly. Now let's get on with the lost dog report. I'm Sergeant Frasier MacKenzie." Ross realized the reply meant the man wasn't about to talk further on the subject.

"Thanks for taking an interest, Sergeant." Ross felt suddenly embarrassed by bringing a lost dog report to the man. He probably had lots of more serious stuff to deal with.

"Story, please." But Sergeant MacKenzie wasn't smiling or scoffing it off.

Ross explained what had happened. When he'd finished, Sergeant MacKenzie told him to wait while he spoke to the officer on duty.

"We'll put out an all-points bulletin for our patrol vehicles to watch for her," he said when he returned. "I'll also alert my wife, Emma. She has a lot of connections in the community, and she's a devoted dog fancier. She'll be more than happy to help. Best I can do. Leave your phone number, and any other way you can be reached, with the officer at the desk."

"Thanks." Ross stood and held out his hand. "Much appreciated."

He started toward the desk but turned back. He had to ask.

"Your shirt…" He pointed to it.

"A gift from Emma." The sergeant grinned. "Last evening was our anniversary. She…we have a Pug named Bruiser. I know, I know. It's a bit over the top for anyone hoping to command any sort of respect, but I do work undercover most of the time, and who'd suspect anyone wearing something like this of being a police officer? Are you married?"

"No."

"Ah, well, then you don't yet understand what a man will sometimes do in the name of love." He headed toward the reception desk. "Something, hopefully, you'll learn one day. We'll be in touch."

Chapter Nine

Bloody hell! No, it can't be.

For the second time in less than a week Ross Turner opened his back door to find Jessi Wallace standing in a downpour, soaked to the skin. As he stood staring out at her, a ragged bolt of lightning illuminated both of them with an intensity much greater than the overhead bulb he'd snapped on.

"*How* did you get here?" The words came on a sharp intake of breath as a boom of thunder all but obliterated them.

"Via a one-way, non-refundable ticket to Calgary." She pushed past him into the kitchen as lightning again brightened the sky and thunder rolled. "I had to walk from the road. My driver wouldn't venture down your trail in this weather."

"Ah, man!" He slammed the door shut behind her, exasperation radiating from every bit of his tone and body. "I thought it was only cats that always came back!"

"Is that all you've got to say?" She followed him as he turned and limped toward a cupboard.

"Best I can come up with." He reached inside and took out a quart of whisky. "You're back, and you'll have to stay…at least until morning. I can't leave you wandering around in a storm."

"I assure you any wandering around in a storm

wasn't something I planned to do when we left here this morning." Then, "Wow!" as she gazed around the kitchen at the gleaming electric range and the washer/dryer pair.

"Don't pretend you're surprised." He splashed whisky into two glasses. "You know my mother is behind this, probably after your description of our living conditions. A truck with these appliances and an installation guy arrived shortly after I got home from Moncton. It also brought two mattresses, a couple of box springs, and an assortment of bedding. It's all in the parlor." Sarcasm reeked from every word.

"Ross, I didn't ask your mother to do any of this." She looked up at him, eyes wide. "She simply asked about the condition of the house, and…"

"And you gave her a glowing description of how her boy was living like a bum. Here." He thrust the glass at her, annoyance such as he believed he'd never before experienced gnawing at his gut.

Why did she have to come back? And why does she have to look so damned sexy, soaking wet and hot with anger?

"Drink up." As she took it, he hoped he sounded disgusted. "It's the best I can do. No friendly neighbor dropped by with more seafood chowder or even a bowl of chicken soup."

"I don't have the time or energy for this." She swallowed the whisky in a single gulp and choked. He knew he should have patted her on the back, but touching her, under the circumstances, wasn't something he wanted to risk. "Right now, I need dry clothes and a warm bed…or mattress. I'll spar with you in the morning."

"Okay, okay." He downed his drink and went back to the cupboard to pour himself another. "Good night."

She started for the front of the house, then stopped.

"Where's Fox?" she asked, looking around.

"I don't know." He uncapped the bottle.

"What do you mean, you don't know?" Her words reeked of total exasperation. "She's your dog, your responsibility! And there's a vicious storm outside, in case you haven't noticed!"

"Look, it was an accident, okay?" He swung back to face her. "After I got home from Moncton and digested all this stuff that had arrived courtesy of my mother, I realized I was nearly out of beer, so I headed for Carleton. I took Fox with me." He went on to tell the story of Fox's disappearance.

"Oh, Ross, no!"

"Yeah, well…"

"I'm so sorry! Did you contact the RCMP and Animal Control?"

"Of course. I'm lame, not stupid!" *God, I'm losing it, snapping at her like that.*

He looked down at the second drink cradled in his hand.

The phone rang out above another flash of lightning and roll of thunder. They started simultaneously. When Ross answered it, Jessi was at his elbow.

"Ross Turner here."

He paused to listen.

"Yeah, well, thanks anyway." He replaced the receiver and stood staring into space.

"They'll find her." Jessi looked up at him. "I know they will."

"Sure."

****

"Would you care to tell me how you got back here?" He joined her in the parlor a half hour later to find her dressed in her horse-pictures pajamas and ensconced on one of the mattresses neatly made up with the new bedding. Across the room the other mattress lay similarly prepared for the night.

"Good old-fashioned resourcefulness."

"Specifics." He sank into the chair that had been his bed, whisky glass in hand.

"So you can avoid making the same mistake again? Well, let me tell you, cowboy, your charm can only be stretched so far. Wine and roses and slow dancing won't work a second time."

"Come on. I'm not that devious…or dumb."

"Really?" Green eyes narrowing, Jessi looked over at him. "So you admit your getting cleaned up and the rest of it was all a ploy to get me to go to Moncton with you, to leave with no choice but to go back to Calgary?"

"Some of it." *And that's the truth.* "So tell me, how did you manage to get back here?"

"Let's just say the barter system is alive and well in New Brunswick." She adjusted her pillow.

"I can see that's all I'm going to get out of you right now, so I may as well leave it there."

"You've got that right."

"And since we now have these almost civilized sleeping quarters, I see no reason for me to continue to sleep in my clothes."

Watching for her reaction, he stood and placed his drink on the mantel. Balancing himself against it, he began to unbutton his shirt.

"Sounds like a good idea. Pleasant dreams, cowboy."

With a disgusted grunt, he pulled off his shirt and jerked open his belt buckle.

Okay, Miss Calm and Cool, I'm going right down to the underwear.

But she'd rolled over, putting her back to him.

Chapter Ten

He was gone from his mattress when she awoke the following morning. Remembering his taunt about getting undressed for bed, she grinned. Seeing a cowboy in his underwear wouldn't have been all that shocking. Still, this was Ross...

The smell of coffee attracted her, and she pulled herself from the mattress and headed barefoot in her flannelette pajamas to the kitchen.

"Smells good." She glanced at Ross, fully clothed, nursing a cup of coffee as he sat at the table.

"This isn't a frat house." He shot her a scowl as she crossed the room to the cupboard to take out a mug. "You could get dressed before putting in an appearance."

"Ah, but you were the first to shatter any and all dress codes, last night." She poured steaming dark brew into her cup and favored him with a sly, taunting glance.

"Here's your wallet." He shoved the leather folder he'd been holding in his left hand across the table toward her. "Everything is there."

"I fully expected it would be." She left it where it was.

"Yeah? You mean in spite of what I tried to do to you, you don't think I'd rifle through your personal stuff?"

"No, that thought didn't cross my mind. You're not that kind of man. Remember, I've known you from 'way back, Ross. Any news about Fox?"

"No."

"Sorry."

****

Jessi, dressed in jeans and sweatshirt, was tidying the kitchen after breakfast when Ross's cell rang.

Please, please let that be good news about Fox. She watched his face as he wrenched it from his pocket and answered.

"Yeah, this is Ross Turner." A pause while he listened, and then his words broke into a burst. "She did? Great, good. Thanks, Sergeant. I'm coming right over."

"Ross, what is it?"

"The wife of an RCMP sergeant and her Pug found Fox," he breathed as he replaced the receiver on its charger. "She's been injured, probably hit by a car. They've taken her to Dr. Masters' clinic at her farm."

"Oh, my God! Ross, wait for me." She dropped the dishcloth and started after him as he stumped toward the door.

"Hurry up!"

She had to run across the yard to keep up with his long, unsteady strides as they headed for his truck. She barely had time to jump into the passenger seat and reach for her seatbelt before he'd revved the engine and was turning the truck toward the lane to the road.

"Whoa, slow down, cowboy!" Jessi bounced against the seatbelt as he drove over the rough road, hitting ruts and roots hard. "Getting us stuck or smashing something on these fancy wheels won't help."

"Okay, okay!" He eased up on the gas, but his hands clutching the wheel were white-knuckled.

He loves that little dog. The realization brought a warm wave washing over Jessi. The accident hadn't entirely turned his heart to stone.

****

At the sign proclaiming the place to be Ebony M Farm, Ross swung the truck into the drive so violently Jessi was again tossed against the limits of her seatbelt.

"Ross, take it easy!"

"Look, I didn't ask you to come along. Furthermore, I don't appreciate backseat drivers."

"Okay, fine." She heaved a deep breath of relief as he braked to a stop in front of a beautifully restored Victorian farmhouse. Painted white, with gingerbread trim, it was exactly the kind of place Jessi admired. The only flaw in the ambience was a built-on section on its side. A sign above its door declared it to be Dr. Shelby Masters' Veterinary Clinic.

As Ross and Jessi got out of the truck, a weathered-looking, rail thin man past middle age came out of the house's front door onto a veranda littered with plastic toys. A small golden-haired cherub trotted after him. In jeans and T-shirt, the little girl had a smile across her rosy-cheeked face.

What a sweetie. A responding smile automatically curled Jessi's own lips.

"Mr. Turner?" the man addressed Ross.

"Yeah. I understand you have my dog here." Jessi heard the words coming out cool and unemotional, but she knew Ross, knew how he hated public emotional outbursts.

"That's right, sir. Doc and her husband are

operating on her right now." He shoved the baseball cap back on his head to scratch his balding head. "Come up on the porch and take a seat. I'm guessin' you'll want to wait around for the results. Just mind the toys. Katie Rose, you're going to have to learn to put that stuff away when you're done playin' with it." He turned to the little girl, who only broadened her smile and caught at his calloused hand.

"Pony, Uncle Grady."

"Well, now, honey, your mom and dad want me to get coffee for these folks." He looked down at the child, and Jessi recognized tender tolerance in his expression. "Maybe later."

A small lower lip pouted out.

"We've had more than enough coffee already, but thanks." She smiled. "But you could take Katie Rose and Ross down to the barn to look over the stock. Katie Rose can show Ross that pony she mentioned. Katie Rose?" She spoke to the child whose expression was brightening at the suggestion. "Ross is a cowboy. He knows lots about horses and ponies. I'll wait here." She looked over at Ross, who was scowling at her. "The minute there's any news, I'll run down and get you."

"Sure would appreciate your opinion on some of the stock, Mr. Turner." The man appeared to have caught her ploy to relieve some of Ross's stress. "I know your reputation."

"Okay, okay." Ross heaved a deep breath and took a firmer grip on his cane.

"Oh, by the way, I'm Grady Wilson." The man held out a work-hardened right hand toward Jessi, while Katie Rose, now dancing with anticipation, clung to his left. "Mr. Turner and I have already met. I took some seafood chowder over to him a few days back."

"A pleasure to meet you, Mr. Wilson." She accepted the offer. "And I assume this is Katie Rose…maybe Dr. Masters' daughter?"

"Yep." He looked down at the child, his fondness glowing out of his sun-bronzed face. "Hers and Jake's…the doc's husband. She's four going on twelve."

"Hi." The child grinned up at her. "But I'm almost five." She held up fingers.

"Nice to meet you, Katie Rose." A startling sense of envy enveloped Jessi. Shelby Masters-Brooks had it all…a career, this lovely place, a husband who shared in her work, and this beautiful child.

Now where did that come from?
****

"Katie Rose, wait up!" Grady Wilson yelled after the little girl scampering down the road ahead of them. "Lots of mud around after yesterday's rain"—he turned to Ross, limping by his side—"and that kid could find a puddle in a desert."

An involuntary grin pulled at Ross's mouth. Something about the little figure scurrying ahead of them lessened the tightness in his chest. He liked kids, always had enjoyed their naturalness, their unprejudiced outlook. And now he was going to be an uncle. He'd get to enjoy one that was almost his own. But it would be a damned long time before he had any himself. Maybe never. What woman would be willing to marry a lame has-been?

They arrived at the paddock beside the barn, and Grady stopped to catch Katie Rose by the hand as she made a dash toward the locked gate. Four horses and a pinto pony stood inside.

"Pretty!" She looked up at Ross and pointed proudly at the pony.

"Pretty?" Ross glanced over at Grady.

"Yeah, well, I reckon it ain't much of a name, but that's what she was dead set on callin' it, so Shelby and Jake went along." He grinned, his nut-brown face crinkling into dozens of element-induced lines, familiar to Ross on all the aging cowboys he'd known. A comfortable sense of being at home settled over him. He liked Grady Wilson…and this place and the horses and the little girl.

"The pretty charcoal mare with the silver mane and tail is the doc's horse, Fancy. The sorrel is the main training horse for beginning riders. Her name is Candy. Great, patient little gal. The big black gelding is Midnight Brandy. He belongs to the doc's brother, Travis. He can give a rider a bit of a challenge if he isn't shown who's boss right off. Our stud Midnight Black is in the barn. He's hot after Candy, so he's penned up."

"That big albino gelding looks pretty fine." Ross turned his attention to the snow-white animal that had come to the fence to nuzzle the wrangler. "He seems fond of you."

"We have a history." Grady rubbed the horse's nose affectionately. "I used to be a wrangler on movie sets. Silver, here, was an actor in a lot of films. I trained him."

"How did the pair of you end up here?"

"Ah, well, long story. Sometime over a beer, maybe. Come on." He took Katie Rose by the hand. "I'll introduce you to our stud. He's quite the boy."

As Grady Wilson led the way through the well-kept stable to a steel-barred box stall at the end, Ross drew a deep breath.

Damn, it's good to be back in a barn, to smell horses and hay...and all the rest of it.

"Here's the lad." Grady stopped in front of the bars behind which a coal black stallion stood, pawing and snorting. "He hasn't had much training lately, what with Travis on the road and him the only one who can put him through his paces. Jake rides him once in a while, but he don't have the know-how to train a big bugger...excuse me, Katie Rose...a big fella like the Black."

"The Black?" Ross stared through the bars at the stallion.

Damn, but he's one magnificent piece of horse flesh. Riding him would be something to remember.

"Well, his name is Midnight Black, but we all just call him the Black."

"Black bad." Katie Rose, in Grady's arms pointed to the stallion.

"Now, missy, that's not right." Grady placed her on her feet on the stable floor. "He's just a big, strong guy who hasn't been getting enough training."

"Pretty, Grady, Pretty." The little girl pulled on his hand.

"Guess I'll have to go saddle up that pony." Grady grinned. "All right, all right, Black," he soothed the stallion as the animal began to half-rear and snort. "I'll play some tunes for you." He reached to a shelf on the wall by the stall and snapped on a dusty CD player. The moment the strains of a country western ballad issued from it, the horse quieted, snorted softly, and settled down, apparently to listen.

"What's that all about?" Ross couldn't disguise his amazement.

"No one understands it." Grady grinned and shook his head. "Travis discovered the big guy had a soft spot for the music of Jordan Brooks a few years back. It's the only thing that never fails to quiet him."

"Can't say I blame him." Ross returned the wrangler's grin. "I was a big fan of Jordan Brooks. Almost got to meet him once at a rodeo in Wyoming."

"Oh, yeah?" Grady shot Ross a look he couldn't interpret before the older man let the child lead him out of the barn toward the paddock.

****

Jessi jumped to her feet as Shelby Masters, wearing blue scrubs, came out onto the veranda.

"Tell me."

"It was touch-and-go for a bit, but now it looks much better." The vet drew a deep breath.

"So Fox will be okay?"

"I don't want to be overly optimistic, but it appears promising." Shelby turned to smile at the tall, handsome man, similarly dressed, who came out of the house to join her. "Thanks, Jake. As always, you did great."

"I managed, Shel, but I don't think I'll ever get over being 'way too empathetic with your patients." He grinned down at her, and she put a hand on his arm.

"Jessi, I'd like you to meet my husband and unofficial vet tech." Shelby turned to her. "Jake Brooks. Jake, this is Jessi Wallace. I told you about her. She's staying with Ross Turner out at the old farm down the road."

"Nice to meet you, Jessi." He stuck out a hand. "We've heard about you. A miracle worker with traumatized horses, right? We had one here a few years back that could have used your help. Remember Grey Lady, Shel?"

"Definitely. Injured in a vehicle accident. She finally came around, but if you'd been available it probably would have taken a lot less time and experimentation to find what worked for her."

"Sometimes a reputation gets blown out of proportion." Jessi hoped she wasn't going to blush. "Now I'd better get down to the barn and tell Ross it looks hopeful for his girl. He doesn't like to show his feelings, but I know he loves that little dog. She's been good therapy for him since he came here."

"Go." Shelby turned to go back into the house. "I feel the need for some very hot, very strong coffee. Coming, Jake?"

"Sure." He paused. "Jessi, I'd like to meet Ross. I used to be around the rodeo circuit years ago. He's a living legend."

"Were you a performer?" Surprised, Jessi looked up at him and something in those blue eyes, broad shoulders, and suntanned face brought a vague sense of recognition.

"Sort of. Let's go, Shel. We have a lot to do yet today, and that coffee might just set us up."

Why is he so anxious to leave when I asked a simple question? Shelby headed for the barn, wondering.

****

Ross was watching Katie Rose, mounted on Pretty, circling the round pen beside the barn, Grady's hand on the bridle, when Jessi's voice made him turn. She was striding toward him and was it…? Yes, definitely—her face was bright and smiling.

"Ross!" she yelled. "Fox is out of surgery! Doctor Masters is optimistic!"

All but running, he began to stumble up the lane to meet her. When he met her, she caught him by the arm, her expression putting a sunrise to shame.

"Ross, Shelby says it looks good," she said. "Fox will need a lot of rest and care, but…"

"Who gives a damn!" Overwhelmed with relief, he shrugged her off and continued on his way, stumping as fast as the cane would allow.

On the veranda of the house, he was greeted by the couple, still in scrubs, coffee cups in hands. The woman he assumed was the vet, the tall man by her side probably her husband. Something about the man seemed vaguely familiar, but he shrugged it aside in his concern for his dog.

"Mr. Turner, I'm Dr. Shelby Masters, and this is my husband, Jake Brooks." She held out a hand.

"Good to meet you, Doc." Ross could barely contain his impatience long enough to accept the introduction. "How's Fox?"

"Doing well, considering." The doctor—he was only slowly coming to recognize what a beautiful woman she was—indicated one of the lawn chairs on the veranda. "Please sit down."

"I'm fine. I'll stand." Balking at her suggestion and only afterwards realizing it had probably simply been a polite invitation, not a concession to his disability, he leaned his hips against the railing.

"Okay." The doctor took a seat, with Jessi

following her. Jake Brooks opted to take up a stance not far from Ross, against a supporting post.

"Tell me." Ross looked squarely at the doctor.

"Sergeant Frasier MacKenzie's wife found Fox in a ditch near the lane that leads to your farm." Shelby pushed a stray curl back into her ponytail. "Well, Emma MacKenzie said it was actually her Pug Bruiser that found her. Fox had apparently been struck by a car when she was trying to get back to you."

"Jesus! I didn't see her. I drove up and down that road a dozen times."

"It may not have happened until some time after you lost her," Jake Brooks offered. "It would have taken her quite a while to get that far from Carleton. Don't beat yourself up."

"Yeah, okay, that could be the case. Still, God only knows how long she lay in that ditch…"

"Ross, it won't help to dwell on it." Jessi looked over at him, and he saw genuine compassion in her eyes.

"Jessi is right," Shelby said. "What is important now is that she's safe and well cared for."

"Can I see her?" Ross levered himself upright.

"I think it best there's as little noise and confusion as possible around her just now," the vet replied. "Although she's sedated, she may still sense what's going on. If she guesses someone she cares about is nearby, it could lead to overstimulation."

"Fine, okay. Whatever you think is best, Doc." He turned to the other woman.

"Come on, Jess. We'll be going."

"I assume our daughter has seduced our wrangler into letting her ride her pony?" Jake Brooks grinned as they turned to leave.

"Yeah, they're down at the round pen."

"Minx." Shelby's tone was tinged with good nature. "Jake, once you've changed out of those scrubs, will you go down and take over? Grady has lots of work to do that doesn't include leading a pony around a ring with a determined four-year-old on its back."

"Sure." He paused and grinned over at Ross. "I've got to tell you, it's a pleasure to meet you. I watched you perform at rodeos and, for sure, I wasn't the least bit surprised when you were named world champion."

"High praise." Ross shuffled his feet. "Thanks."

"Jake." Shelby, apparently sensing Ross's discomfort, jerked her head in the direction of the house. "Grady? Katie Rose?"

"Right. Better get to it. Nice to meet you folks."

Chapter Eleven

Ross pulled into a convenience store and hobbled inside. Shortly he emerged with two Styrofoam cups of coffee. He stopped at the passenger door and offered one in to her.

"I thought we could both use a drink." His expression had relaxed, and there was even a hint of a grin at the corners of his lips and eyes.

"Thanks." She took the cup and let a bit of a smile flicker up at him.

He returned to the driver's seat, leaned forward to start the engine, then fell back with a sigh. His hand dropped from the key in the ignition to his thigh.

"Look, Jessi, I'm sorry about the trick I pulled on you in Moncton." He stared out the windshield into the sunlight, avoiding her eyes. "You didn't deserve to be treated that way."

"It was pretty awful," she said gravely. "A first-class ticket to Calgary."

He turned sharply to look at her, but she was staring out the front window, the glare of morning sunshine only half disguising the fact that her lips were twitching upwards at the corners.

"Yeah, well…" He gave up and started the engine. But as he turned back onto the highway and pulled down the sun visor, he asked, "How did you manage to get back to the farm? You never did explain…exactly."

"I swapped that one-way ticket for a one-way drive in a delivery van to Carleton."

"Mom said you were resourceful. She just didn't add extremely. Is that a purely unique trait, or is it inherited?"

"Runs in the family."

"I guess I knew that."

"Just drive…into Carleton, please."

"Why?"

"I want to do some shopping."

"I already did."

"Yes, and I appreciate your efforts even if the motive behind it was part of your plot to get rid of me." She settled more comfortably into the seat. "But I need some other items."

"Oh."

"Oh?" She looked over at him, eyes narrowing. "What does that mean?"

"Well, that would explain why you were so cranked up when you got back to the farm yesterday."

"Oh, for God's sake, Ross! I don't need to buy feminine hygiene products! Why does every man on the planet seem determined to attribute a woman's annoyance with them to time of the month and not simply their own irritating behavior? I'm talking about detergent for that new washer and fabric sheets for the dryer, as well as some other stuff."

"Okay, okay, heading for Carleton…not to purchase any female products."

****

Jessi came out of the supermarket pushing a cart full of plastic bags and began to load them into the back seat of the king cab.

"Need some help?" Involved in listening to country tunes on the radio, Ross glanced casually over his shoulder.

"No, thank you."

"Okay. Will you just listen to this Jordan Brooks tune? Man, he was the greatest. Wonder whatever became of him?"

"Probably got laryngitis, gave up, and hermited himself away in a farmhouse somewhere."

"Nasty."

"Yes, well, if the comparison fits…" She turned away to put the cart into the corral beside the truck.

****

"Lunch." Jessi came out onto the front veranda of the farmhouse where he'd been watching sunlight dancing off the waves of a beautiful autumn day. He'd been surprised to find he was actually finding some pleasure in the ambience.

"Okay." He punched off on his cell phone and turned to see her carrying a tray of food.

"Calling a friend?"

"No one I've ever met. Emma MacKenzie. I needed to thank her…and her dog…for finding Fox."

"That was thoughtful…and necessary."

She placed a pair of plates, each bearing thick sandwiches, on the old table's surface. Then she added two tall glasses of milk and a couple of bananas.

"Ah, come on!" He glared at the meal. "Monkey food? And that white stuff in the glasses is intended for calves. This is what you were dead set on buying? Feminine hygiene products would have been better than this."

"Come on, cowboy." She took a chair at the table

and waved a hand to indicate the place opposite. "Where's your sense of adventure? Afraid of a little genuine nutrition?"

"Not of nutrition, but, hell, this looks like a page out of Canada's food guide."

"Oh, stop bellyaching. I could have served you a big bowl of kale."

"What's kale?"

"Good lord!" She heaved an exasperated groan.

"Hell of a thing, when a man can't even pick his own food." He moved to take the chair and sat down harder than he'd intended. The force made him flinch.

"You okay?"

"Fine, fine." In an effort to divert attention from the incident, he picked up a section of sandwich and took a bite.

"Not half bad, is it?" She grinned over at him as he chewed.

"It's okay," he muttered. He'd liked clubhouse sandwiches when he was a kid. Now the old taste he'd had for them returned, but he wasn't about to let her see it.

"I remember my mom making them for you and Chase that spring you came over to help out with the branding. Janet was staying with us, too, helping out."

"Yeah?"

"Yeah. You sound surprised."

"You were a kid back then. I thought you and my future sister-in-law were too busy with teenage crushes and hair styles to notice a couple of dusty, dirty cowhands that were too old for you, never mind notice what they ate."

"I was young, not unobservant."

"Huh." Hell, she was always besting him. He'd eat the damned sandwich, drink that miserable milk, and even force down that blasted banana.

I'll show her I can stomach any forage she can throw my way.

He refused to acknowledge he was enjoying the lunch.

"When did you discover the tickets in your purse?" He paused between bites to ask the question that had been nagging at him since she'd returned but which Fox's accident had put on hold.

"When I was about to buy a coffee at the hotel."

"Aha. That would have presented a problem."

"Yes, it did, but it also gave me an opportunity to swap that ticket for a ride to Carleton and even out along the coast road to your lane."

"Resourceful."

"Yes, I am. And don't you forget it."

Her cell rang, and she answered. "Dad?"

He continued to eat but couldn't help overhearing.

"Yes, I'm fine. Beautiful day here. You should see the beach and bay. Lovely place for a vacation." She paused to listen, her face crumbling from the delight it had registered on recognition of her father's voice, her tone changing to one of agitation.

"I didn't think he'd have the nerve to show up at the ranch again after that last encounter with you. Dad...Dad, listen to me...Kicking him so far he'd land on his backside in Montana isn't the answer...No, I certainly don't want him back, but I don't want him mutilated, either." Another pause, then, "Good. I'm glad Mom was on hand to be the voice of reason. I'm sure he won't bother you again."

Again she listened and looked over at Ross, rolling her eyes. "Yes, Dad, I'm fine, Ross is fine. He's being a perfect gentleman. There'll be no need for you to polish up your boot to kick his behind… Okay, love you, love to Mom. See you both soon."

She ended her call and returned to her meal.

"What?" She glanced up to catch him looking at her.

"Nothing, nothing." He returned his attention to his food. "Just can't help wondering who it is your father is wanting to either kick into the good ol' US of A or permanently alter physically."

"I'm surprised you don't know who he was talking about."

"Not a clue."

"It's Clint Harrison."

"Jesus. You weren't involved with *him*?" His head lurched up.

"You sound surprised. No, scratch that. Shocked."

"Yeah, well, I had you figured for a nice girl, not one of those buckle bunnies Harrison runs around with."

"I wasn't a buckle bunny!" Her face contorted with outrage. "I was his fiancée."

"Oh, God." In an effort to avoid looking at her, he returned his attention to his sandwich.

Silence. He took a drink of milk.

"I'm glad you said 'was,' " he said finally. "Clint Harrison is a certifiable bum where women are concerned."

She suppressed a giggle.

"That's a change of pace."

"It's difficult to stay annoyed with a man sporting a

milk mustache." She chuckled and handed him a napkin. "Here."

"Glad it amused you." He wiped his mouth. "Losing Harrison doesn't deserve wasting a minute on regret. You couldn't have been around the rodeo circuit much or you'd have known his reputation."

"No, I wasn't. I met Clint when he came out to our ranch to buy a horse." She watched her finger making absentminded circles on the table beside her plate. "He…had a way about him. We dated a few times while he was in the area, and then we called and texted a lot last winter while he was on the southern circuit. This spring he arrived at the ranch in early May with a ring and a proposal. My parents seemed to like him, and he really liked the ranch. He said it was just the kind of place he hoped to settle down on one day. When he went back on the circuit, I was confident he loved me and would be faithful." She paused to draw a deep breath.

Ross sat silent, and she continued. "It was a fluke that I ended up at the rodeo where you and he were both performing. I went down there to deliver a horse I'd been training back to its owner. I knew Clint was performing at the show. I planned to surprise him with a visit. After your accident, I forgot about my original idea and rushed out to his trailer to see if he had any news about your condition. I found him half naked and holding an equally half naked woman in his arms."

"Damn!" Ross pulled himself up in his chair and threw his napkin onto the table. "Rotten bastard. Still, about what I'd expect from him." Seeing the hurt in Jessi's eyes, he softened his tone. "Good part is you found out what he is before you married the bum."

"I guess." She stared down at her half-eaten lunch.

"Look." He leaned toward her and struggled to find the right words. "I know it must have hurt like a bash in the head. But trust me, you'll find a better man. And"— he straightened back on his chair and picked up a triangle of sandwich—"knowing Clint Harrison, it shouldn't be all that hard." He let a grin quirk the corner of his mouth. When he glanced over at her, he caught the glimmer of a smile quivering on her lips.

"Furthermore…" He decided to press his advantage. "I wouldn't want to be in his boots right now. Jack Wallace was a bulldogger before he retired from the rodeo circuit, wasn't he?"

Jessi nodded. "Won a few championships, in fact."

"Yeah, I remember. Not a man I'd want to tangle with, even if he is a few years older. If Harrison is stupid enough to show up around your father, he just might find himself making landfall somewhere south of the border."

"He already did and narrowly escaped the trip you just described."

Their gazes met and both grinned.

****

"Ross?" Jessi came back out onto the veranda after she'd finished cleaning up the lunch dishes to find him lying on the swing.

"What now?" He looked up at her from beneath half-opened lids. "Is it time for my calisthenics? Or maybe it's yoga? Either way, the answer is a big fat no."

"Back to being the Grinch That Stole September, are we? What would make you think I'd suggest either? Ross, you've got to stop suspecting me of constantly

118

trying to do something for your own good." She grinned. "In case you didn't get it, that was a joke."

"I got it, I got it." He pulled himself to a sitting position. "Look, I'm sorry as hell about the way Harrison treated you, but I'm not about to let you boss me around or make me do anyone's bidding but my own to try to compensate for that useless piece of trash."

"Fine. I get it. So we're back to going one on one."

"I'd hardly say that, but…"

"Oh, for heaven's sake, stop trying to play with words. It's a beautiful afternoon. I think we should take that old boat and go out to explore that island over there." She indicated the small bit of land about a quarter mile off shore.

"There's nothing to explore. It's a glorified sandbar with a few straggling black spruce and a whole lot of chest-high marsh grass."

"Come on." She slapped the baseball cap she'd been carrying onto her head. "It'll pass the time. No sense sitting here and brooding about Fox. She's in good hands."

"I'm not brooding about a stray mutt. Okay, okay." He pushed himself to his feet. "I can see I'll get no peace if I don't agree. I'll change into shorts. I have a feeling we're going to get more than our feet wet in that old tub."

As he went into the house, Jessi let a satisfied smile tip her lips.

Okay, cowboy, the game is definitely on. Prepare for your first major dose of therapy.

"I'll go down the shore and push the boat into the water," she called after him.

The reply was a grunt.

****

"Isn't it lovely out on the water, Ross?" Jessi sat in the back of the old boat and trailed her fingers in the water while he rowed toward the island. "Aren't you glad we came?"

"I'd be a lot more glad if you'd stop dragging your hand," he muttered. "Rowing this old tub is hard enough without your holding it back. And by the way, I didn't appreciate your putting your arm around me to help me into the boat."

"Sorry." She raised her fingers and smiled at him, trying not to let her gaze drop to his left leg and the massive scar running nearly the full length of it to disappear into the khaki shorts he wore. She'd been startled when he'd arrived at the shore and his clothing for the first time had allowed her to see his wound. When he'd undressed for bed at night she'd turned her back, and in the morning he was up before she awoke. This had been her first major look at the aftermath of his injury, and she'd had to stifle her shock under a quick intake of breath and a bright smile.

My God, I had no idea it was that bad.

"Look." He paused and rested the oars on the gunwales. "There's no use pretending you don't notice the scar, that it doesn't freak you out. Let's be honest. It is ugly as sin."

"It's a sports injury." She wasn't about to let him get her to admit she was appalled. "Nothing to get riled up about. Lots of cowboys have battle scars. It's a rough life. Goes with the territory."

"Huh." He took up the oars and heaved toward the island. "That's quite a philosophy."

"It's only the truth. Oh, look, Ross! A flock of herring gulls overhead. Did you know that, although a lot of people call them sea gulls, there's no such species, that they're actually herring gulls? Lots of other types of sea birds are native to this area, too. I read about them on the plane coming out here."

"Yeah, well, see how wonderful you think they are when they start dropping all over us."

"The Grinch of September!" She leaned back in the boat and fell silent.

When they reached the island, Jessi helped Ross pull their craft up into the grass.

"Let's take a walk to the far side," she suggested as Ross placed the oars under the seats. "I'll bet you can see forever, out across the water over there."

"Not forever, just Quebec, and only on a clear day. You're not going to be looking out across the Atlantic. This is Chaleur Bay."

"Okay, Quebec will do just fine. In fact, it will be much better than miles and miles of blank ocean. Come on." She started off through the grass. When she heard no sound to indicate he was following her, she turned back. "Ross, move it." Her tone sharpened.

"Damn it, you sound like a drill sergeant." His response was a mutter as he took up his cane and began to stump after her.

She grinned as expletives marked his following her through the ragged marsh grass.

"Oh, darn!"

"What now?" Annoyance colored the word.

"I forgot my sunglasses in the boat. I'll have to go back for them. You keep going. I'll catch up."

"Sure, sure." He pushed past her. "I won't get far

ahead, right?"

For a moment she watched him go, then shrugged and headed back to the boat.

So far, so good. He hasn't checked for his cell. I'm amazed I was able to sneak it out of his pocket so easily when I pretended to help him into the boat.

****

"Look." She came out of the stand of straggly black spruce into waist-high marsh grass and pointed. "That must be Quebec. Beautiful through that bluish haze. Much better than having discovered the Atlantic." She tossed a grin back over her shoulder at him.

"Yeah, yeah." He sank down on a driftwood log and rested his cane against it.

She pulled two chocolate bars from the pocket of her shorts and handed one to him.

"What's this?" He squinted up at her in the sunlight.

"Energy food. Just the thing to shore a person up on a hike."

"I was expecting granola…or fruit." He took one from her and began to peel away the wrapper.

"Hey, I'm not beyond the odd bit of fun food. You underestimate me, mister."

"I don't think so."

"If you're referring to that night on the veranda…" This time it was her words that reflected annoyance.

"Sorry about that." He bit into the bar. "Guess I was trying to prove myself."

"And gain my confidence so you could pull that trick on me the next day." The anger she'd been controlling burst out. "Good God, Ross!"

"Yeah, well, maybe it was more than that."

"More than that? What more than that could there possibly be?" She stood, legs shoulder-width apart, arms crossed on her chest, and faced him.

"I guess I was trying to find out if I still had what it took to interest a lady." He looked up at her, eyes squinting in the sunlight coming from behind her.

"So you decided to prove yourself by making a play for me. Ross, that's despicable."

"Yeah, I guess, but when you're dragging a gimpy leg and not sure…"

He glanced to the left into the trees.

"Not sure you could make love?" Her tone softened as she turned back.

"In flowery terms, yeah."

"But you stopped short. Why?"

He didn't answer right away. When he did, he focused on the sand under his feet.

"Because you're Jess. Checking myself out with you would just be wrong."

She didn't reply. For a few moments there was only the soughing of the soft breezes through the ragged spruce and swaying marsh grass.

"Thank you." The two words came out softly. He looked up at her, and their gazes locked.

"Enough said." He snapped back into his belligerent character and again bit into his chocolate bar. "How long do we have to sit here enjoying a bunch of blue hills and gray water?" He spoke with his mouth full.

She sighed. Ross the Rude was back.

****

"Ah, bloody hell! Will you look at that? I told you that old tub wasn't seaworthy!"

Ross stared at the rowboat half sunk a few feet off shore.

Jessi stared at the boat, then out across the water.

"The tide must have come in," she said.

"Yeah, yeah, the tide must have come in," he snapped. "Now it's almost twice as far to shore. We'll have to call for help and look like the right pair of fools." His hand went to the back pocket of his shorts. "Ah, damn. My phone must have fallen out somewhere along this ridiculous expedition. Okay, we'll use yours. Give it here." He held out a hand.

She dug into her pockets, then raised empty hands. "I must have left it in the pocket of my jeans."

"Well, isn't this just great! Stranded on an island a quarter mile from the farm at high tide. This mess couldn't have been more complete if it had been orchestrated—ah, hell, it was, wasn't it?" He turned on her. "I'll bet you pushed the boat out to where it would take on water, maybe even shoved a few planks loose when you made that excuse of turning back for your sunglasses. And I'm guessing you swiped my cell when you attempted to help me into the boat."

"Ross…"

"You want me to have to swim back to the farm. This is the same kind of treatment you use with injured horses, right? I've heard about it, so don't deny the fact. Now we're in a fine pickle."

"It's not that far." She put her hands on her hips and squinted toward the dilapidated old house. "It shouldn't take more than a few minutes."

"And what if I can't swim? Did you think of that?"

"Oh, I know you can." She cast him a sly, sideways glance.

"Yeah? How?"

"That year you and Chase came to help with the branding…it was a really hot spring. Do you remember you and your brother cooling off in the swimming hole Dad had dug in the creek down beyond the paddocks?"

"Yeah, so?"

"And that Janet was staying with us?"

"Okay, okay, memories revived. Where is this going?"

"Well, Janet and I were teenagers, curious teenagers, just getting really interested in boys."

"Ah, don't tell me. You sneaked down and watched."

"Well, then I won't. I will say we both got an eyeful…two good-looking guys, skinny-dipping. Maybe it was then Janet started thinking about marrying Chase."

She sauntered toward the shore, shooting him a teasing backward glance over her shoulder. "Come on, cowboy, time to start swimming. Only this time, keep your pants on."

Did anyone ever die of exasperation? If it's possible, I'm a prime candidate.

Chapter Twelve

"Come on, swim! You can do it." She turned back and yelled at him. "We're almost there."

"Doin' the best I can." He fought for breath and calm. *This woman will be the death of me.*

Ahead, he saw her reach water shallow enough to allow her to get to her feet. Standing, she waited for him, waves lapping about her waist.

Bloody hell, in that wet T-shirt...

With what he figured was near the end of his strength, he managed to reach out with long crawl strokes. Shortly, finally, blessedly, he put his feet on a sandy bottom. "Told you you could do it." She grinned triumphantly as he caught at her arm to pull himself upright.

"Yeah, well, lucky for you." The words blurted out in gasps.

"For me?"

"If you'd had to tell my mother you'd drowned me, you'd suffer a fate worse than I had."

"Laura is a pretty darned compassionate person." She smirked back at him. "She would have understood."

He ignored the remark and staggered to shore. A few feet up onto the overgrown lawn, his toe hit something in the grass. Looking down, he saw sunlight glinting off his cell.

"Great!" He bent, suppressing a groan, and picked it up. *Blast the woman!* Grasping it, he continued on toward the house. He was starting up the verandah steps when her voice made him pause.

"Looking good, mister. Made it all the way to the house…without your cane."

Sweet Jesus! I did. Somehow I did. Astounded he stopped dead in his tracks. *The swimming…did that do it?*

A pain shot up his leg, and he grabbed the railing. *No, it was just one of those crazy things you do when you're fighting for your life. Like when you fall off a bull. A major adrenalin rush. If you're conscious, you run like hell to get out of the way, no matter how bad you're hurt.*

He entered the house and headed for the bathroom. A shower. He needed a hot shower. Let her wait. This whole blasted mess had been her doing. He shed his wet clothes and turned on the water.

But as warm water eased away the cold and he relaxed beneath the flow, another thought struck him. He stopped rubbing the soapy washcloth over his chest.

Damn, it feels good to be alive, to have survived under my own power. Even if I ended up panting like an old dog in August. Maybe the woman has the odd good idea.

****

"A real gentleman, aren't you?" Jessi, sitting cross-legged on her mattress and wearing her flannelette pajamas, greeted him as he came out of the bathroom in the robe she'd borrowed her first night at the farm. "You didn't think twice about dashing into the shower ahead of me." Her hair still damp and tangled, she held dry underwear and a gray jogging suit as she glared at him.

"Since you were the reason for our condition, I felt I had dibs. Anyhow, you appear to have gotten out of wet clothes and made yourself comfortable." He limped to the hall closet and reached inside. When his hand emerged, he held a cane.

"Oh, come on!" Exasperation burst from her words. "You just swam a quarter mile and walked almost a hundred yards up from the shore unassisted."

"Yeah, well, desperate situations call for desperate actions." He reached into the closet and fumbled about. When he emerged he held an assortment of dry clothes. "Now my leg hurts like hell, and as soon as I'm dressed, I plan to medicate myself with a couple of beers."

"Argh!" She headed for the bathroom, shoulders squared, annoyance in every stride.

"Lots of hot water left," he called after her. "I'm enough of a gentleman to see that there is."

The door slammed on his words.

****

Jessi came into the kitchen in a gray jogging suit, her hair blown dry, and feeling much better, to find him seated at the table in jeans and gray sweatshirt, nursing a beer.

"No pills accompanying that, I hope?" She went to the refrigerator and helped herself to a long neck.

"I've already told you…I don't do that."

"Just checking."

Her cell rang, and she pulled it from a back pocket.

"Now you find it tucked away…in a jogging suit." He gave her a withering glance, and she smirked back.

"Hello. Shelby? Sure, we'd love to. See you at six."

She punched out and turned to Ross.

"Shelby and Jake have invited us to dinner tonight."

"And you accepted…for both of us? Argh!"

"Oh, come on. You might get to visit Fox. And you'll feel right at home on a horse farm. Anyhow"—she heaved a sigh and sat down opposite—"I need to share a conversation with someone who isn't constantly grumpy and suspicious of my every move."

"So the therapist needs therapy." He watched her through narrowed eyes as she took a pull on her beer.

"Physician, heal yourself." She cocked her head to favor him with a sly grin. "I can't very well help you if I'm tied up in knots myself, can I?" She stood. "Now I'm going out onto the veranda to enjoy this beer and the rest of this lovely afternoon before we have to get dressed to go to Ebony M Farm. You can either join me or sit here in a purple funk."

She picked up her bottle and strode toward the front of the house. As he heard the door bump shut behind her, he muttered an expletive, paused a moment, then grasped his cane and followed.

****

"Shelby, that was absolutely delicious." Jessi heaved a sigh as she finished her serving of apple pie and ice cream in the farmhouse kitchen. "And that lobster salad…wow!"

"Thank you. Sorry the lobster wasn't fresh out of the bay, only from the freezer." The vet stood and began to gather up dishes. "Our season finished at the end of June. The salad was made from some Jake and I

129

froze."

"Nevertheless, it was great." Jessi got up as well. "Let me help you clean up."

"No need, Jessi. You're a guest. I was going to suggest the guys take Katie Rose down to the barn to say goodnight to Pretty. Maybe you'd like to go along?'

"No, thanks. I'll visit the barn another time." She began to gather up dessert plates.

"Come on, Ross." Jake took his daughter out of her booster seat and up into his arms. "We'll go and let the ladies talk." He gave the little girl a quick kiss on the cheek. "Anyhow, this young lady won't even consider going to bed until she hugs that pony goodnight."

Looking from Shelby to Jake and their daughter, Jessi felt a twinge of something she hated to recognize as envy. Happiness. Contentment. Trust. That's what they had, all the chief components of a solid family life. She wondered if she'd have had even one of those with Clint.

****

She and Shelby chatted about their work with horses as they filled the dishwasher and tidied the kitchen.

"How about another coffee in the living room?" the vet suggested as she punched the machine into action. "Knowing Katie Rose's reluctance to leave that pony and go to bed, the guys might be a while."

"Sounds good."

"I hope I'm not talking out of turn." Shelby looked across at Jessi once they were seated in the living room. "But I do know why you're here. It's a lot more than a visit to a friend. You're here to try to help Ross get over his injury…psychologically. When she called me a week ago, Laura Turner confided in me. She felt we had enough in common that we might be able to collaborate."

"You're right." Jessi settled back in the comfortable chair with a sigh. "But I don't seem to be doing much to help at present. About all I've managed so far is to get him to swim." She went on to tell Shelby about their adventure coming back from the island.

Shelby grinned when she'd finished. "That was a bit devious, but warranted. Also, with a good deal of scientific research to back it up…at least, as we both know, with horses. Apparently it had a positive effect. You said he managed to walk without his cane from the beach to the house."

"He did, but as soon as he'd showered and had time to think, he grabbed another one." Jessi heaved a deep breath. "I must say, I was glad to receive your invitation to dinner tonight, for more reasons than one. First, I looked forward to spending time with you and your family. Second, it got Ross out of the house and into a social situation. He needs more interaction with people. I have a feeling that before I came he had some plan to hermit away on the farm and drink himself stupid every night."

"Not good." Shelby shook her head. "But I can understand a bit of your challenges. Jake arrived here sick and disillusioned about six years ago. Added to the problem, I had this huge prejudice against him. At least you aren't struggling under any such feeling."

Jessi looked down into her coffee cup and hesitated.

"Jessi, you can't tell me you came here with any ill feelings against Ross." Shelby's eyebrows raised.

"According to Mrs. Turner, you were childhood friends…or something of the sort."

"We were friends." She spoke slowly. "But Ross is a few years older, which made a giant difference to teenagers. A lot has happened since then. Ross went off on the rodeo circuit, while I built up a business working with traumatized horses. And I got myself involved with a rodeo cowboy who turned out to be heartbreak on the hoof…as I've told you. So, while I might not be prejudiced against Ross himself, I have to admit I have a fair bit of animosity toward rodeo cowboys in general."

"Coming through." Jake's soft words made both women turn toward the kitchen doorway. Shelby's husband entered with a sleepy toddler in his arms, her head on his shoulder. Ross followed. "This young lady fell asleep against a hay bale while Ross and I were talking horses."

"I'll take her up." Shelby started to rise. "She'll need a bath."

"Stay where you are, Mommy." Jake continued on toward the stairs. "You bathed her to within an inch of her life before our guests arrived for dinner. Right now, all she needs is her pajamas, bed, and that ragged stuffed pony. I can see to all that."

"Thanks." Shelby sank back onto the couch, smiling at her husband. "Nightie night, Katie Rose darling," she called out to the drowsy child.

"Nightie night, Mommy."

"Come, join us, Ross." Shelby indicated a chair near the fireplace. "From the looks of our daughter, it won't take Jake long to get her settled. Would you like a fire?" She indicated the hearth with a box with papers, kindling, and logs beside it.

"Wouldn't say no." His face eased into an expression Jessi recognized as the most relaxed of any she'd seen since her arrival. Coming to the Brooks's for dinner had been a good idea. He continued, "Jessi and I had a bit of an adventure this afternoon, and the September waters of Chaleur Bay didn't feel near as warm as they're reputed to be."

"You mean that legend that it was originally called the Bay of Heat?" Shelby chuckled, starting to get up.

"Yeah, that. And you don't have to trouble yourself. I've lighted more than a few fires in my time." He cast Jessi a sly grin that caused her to cast him a sarcastic grimace as he knelt in front of the fireplace.

"Asleep already." Jake came down the stairs as Ross was tossing a match into an arrangement of logs, kindling, and paper in the fireplace. He sank down on the couch beside Shelby and took her hand.

"You should have seen her helping Jake in the vegetable garden this morning." Shelby entwined her fingers with her husband's and chuckled. "She was dirt from head to toe."

"Well, you can't harvest potatoes without getting dirty." Jake grinned, looking over at their guests. "I enjoy my garden…when there's time to work in it."

"Jake's from Prince Edward Island, land of the potato," Shelby said. "You can take the boy off the island, but you can't take potato farming…or lobster fishing…out of his blood."

"Farmer, were you, Jake?" Jessi was pleased to see Ross, the old Ross she'd known years ago, joining easily into the conversation as he'd once done.

"My father is a potato farmer and lobster

fisherman. I grew up farming and fishing. You sound surprised."

"Down at the barn just now, you talked about horses like someone who's been around them for years."

"Shelby has taught me well." He quirked a grin at his wife. "When I came here, I hardly knew which end to put the bridle on."

"Jake works most afternoons at the local high school, counseling at-risk teens." Shelby's abrupt change of subject surprised Jessi. Was there something in her husband's past she didn't want dug up?

"Good for you." Jessi let the thought pass and moved on with the change in conversation. "I've run a few riding clinics for troubled kids, but I have to admit not as many as I'd like. Maybe someday."

Ross, apparently getting comfortable with his companions, settled back into his chair, but as he adjusted his leg he flinched.

"How about a wee dram, as a Scotsman would say, Ross?" Jake stood and indicated a well-stocked bar in one corner. "It used to help me sleep when my leg was giving me grief."

"You hurt your leg?"

"A car accident a few years back." Jake poured two measures into a pair of glasses.

"But you're not limping now."

"Fortunately I made a complete recovery. Nevertheless, I can recall how tiresome walking with a cane can be." He returned to the group and held out the glass to Ross, who paused and looked over at Jessi.

"Go ahead." She nodded. "If Jake says it will help, it's worth a try. I'll drive back to the farm."

"Thanks." Ross accepted the drink and sipped before looking back at Jake, who'd resumed his seat by Shelby. "If you don't mind my asking, how did you manage to…?"

"Get better?" The man turned to grin at his wife. "I got married."

"Jake, you know that's not true! You were recovering quite nicely from the day I asked you to marry me."

"You proposed?" Jessi chuckled. "Bravo, Shelby."

"Well, he'd been making it plain he was more than slightly interested." The vet cast a teasing glance at her husband. "Then he had a car accident during the first snowfall of that winter. He was trying to come back to me through a blizzard, and that told me he was ready to accept my proposal. We were married on Christmas Eve that year."

"How romantic!"

"Yeah, well, I'm not quite ready for that kind of cure." Ross finished his drink and stood. "We'd better get going. These good people are farmers as well as professionals in other lines of work. They need their rest. Thanks for the dinner and"—he raised his empty glass to Jake before replacing it on the bar—"the drink. But before we go…" He hesitated, then voiced the request he'd held burning inside all evening. "Can I see Fox?"

"I think that might be okay." Shelby stood and led the way to the closed clinic door. "But just for a minute. She's still weak, and any excitement…"

"Sure, sure."

As Jessi stood to follow the vet and Ross into the clinic, she let a small smile of satisfaction tip her lips.

This was the first time she'd heard Ross sound eager about anything since she'd arrived.

Fox, you have to get better. You're his one bright spot…apparently.

****

The moment Fox saw Ross enter the clinic, she struggled to get out of her bed in the pen holding it.

"Easy, girl." Ross knelt beside her, and Jessi noticed he barely flinched as he dropped down to be with her. Again, she made a mental wish that the little dog got well soon.

"She's still weak." Shelby stepped forward to release the catch on the pen and let her free. "And she has a fair number of stitches, so take it easy with her." She indicated the swath of bandages around the dog's shoulders.

"Sure, sure." Ross appeared to be only half listening as he crouched on the floor, Fox clambering onto his lap. "You're looking real pretty, girl," he talked to her as Jessi hadn't heard him do previously. "You work hard and get well, so I can take you home."

He looked up questioningly at Shelby as Fox slathered kisses over his face. "When?"

"In a day or so. I want to keep an eye on her for a while yet. And, Ross, I think you should know." The vet paused and glanced at Jessi, then back to the man holding the little dog. "The nerves in her right shoulder have been crushed. She'll most likely always limp."

Silence. *Oh, God.* Jessi held her breath. *Just what Ross didn't need to hear.*

Finally he spoke.

"Okay, well, if that's the worst we have to deal with, we sure as hell can. I've got a lot of experience with that, haven't I, girl? We'll limp along together."

Fox, too happy to be back with him, yelped and tried to scramble closer.

"That's enough for now." Shelby picked up the dog and jerked her head toward the door. "You folks leave while I settle her for the night."

"Sure, whatever you say, Doc." Ross stumbled to his feet but paused to stroke the little canine's head. "You have to stay with the doctor for now, girl, but I'll be back for you real soon."

As Jake, Jessi, and Ross left the clinic, Fox yowled. Ross turned to go back, but Jessi caught his arm.

"Remember what Shelby said, Ross. She has to settle for the night."

"Yeah, yeah, right, sure."

The concern on his face made an astonishing thought flash through Jessi's mind. If the man could be so caring about a little dog, wouldn't he make a good father?

Good God, where did that idea come from?

****

"You do realize they were joking?" Ross looked at Jessi as she turned the truck into the farm's driveway and headed down the lane to the main road.

"About what?" She glanced over at him, glad her eyes were hidden behind mirror sunglasses that protected her from the last blaze of sun setting over the bay in front of them and his scrutiny.

"Don't play innocent." He turned his gaze out through the windshield, squinting against the brightness. He grabbed up his Ray-Bans from the dash and put them on.

"Oh, you mean about their getting married curing

Jake's leg?"

"Exactly."

"Well, you can relax, cowboy. I don't owe your family that much."

"Good. Glad to hear it. After that 'how romantic' remark…"

"I thought Fox looked on the road to recovery." Jessi changed the subject. "It was good to hear we might be able to bring her home in a day or so."

His reply was a grunt. Assuming he wanted to be left in silence, Jessi focused her attention on driving.

At the farmhouse, he got out and limped inside ahead of her.

When she entered the kitchen, he was pouring a measure of whisky into a glass.

"I'm going out on the front veranda for a while." He hoisted the bottle toward her in invitation.

"No, thanks, but I'll join you in watching the moon and stars come out." She followed him to the front of the house.

For a while they sat in silence as the last rays of day vanished across the bay. When a sliver of moon appeared, frogs began to sing from the brook behind the house, and the softness of a warm September night enveloped them.

"Well, aren't you going to say it?" He finally broke the silence.

"Say what?"

"About one whisky being enough."

"Why should I?" She shrugged. "You're home for the night, you won't be driving anywhere."

"What if I have three or four or God knows how many?"

"So, what do you expect me to say? That it wouldn't be a good idea, that I'm ordering you to stop? Well, don't hold your breath."

"Why?"

"You know the old adage about leading a horse to water? The reverse is also true. You can tell someone not to drink, but you can't stop them."

"Just full of psychology, aren't you?" He shot her a look that even in the shadows she could interpret as filled with annoyance.

"I know my way around stubborn cowboys." She turned her gaze out across the bay. For a few moments they sat in silence. "Anyway, why are you so grouchy all of a sudden? I thought you enjoyed the evening. And Fox is getting well."

"Yeah, well, maybe seeing her doomed to stump along like me for maybe the rest of her life, just because I was careless, gave me a royal kick in the conscience."

"It wasn't your fault. She bolted. Dogs do things like that. Now, can we just settle down to enjoy the evening? Do you know the only thing that could be better than this?" She drew a deep breath.

"Being here with anyone but me?"

"Come on, let your grump go. I was going to say being back in Alberta, riding home with the sun setting over the foothills. The leaves on the birches will be turning yellow now and looking like pure gold. There'll be a hint of frost in the air, and the horse will prick up his ears and shake his bridle and trot faster as he realizes he's almost finished for the day. Maybe a coyote will howl or an owl will hoot as the moon appears."

"Yeah." The word coming out of the darkness was

a wheeze of wistfulness.

"Now if you're done second-guessing me, I'll head inside to bed." She stood.

"Damn!"

Before she could be ready for what happened next, he was on his feet and taking her into his arms. The next moment he was kissing her in something that was anything but a friendship kiss.

Oh, God, Ross…

She hadn't been prepared for this. But could anyone be prepared for the way he pulled her tight against him, the way his lips found hers, the way his mouth opened over hers, the way he made her world spin, her entire body awake with desire. Pressed against him, she could have no doubt of his. In those moments, Jessi knew passion as never before. And when he drew back, she was left weak-kneed and dizzy.

"Jess?" He looked down at her. In the moonlight she could see the planes of his face hard with…what? Passion, desire? The pure animal lust of a man without female companionship for too long? No, there'd been too much gentleness involved for it to be the latter. Not like Clint, not like Clint.

In the suddenness of a whiplash, reality struck back strong and hard. An image of another cowboy holding Ginny Morgan in his arms burst into her mind. She lurched free.

"Are you sure you only had two whiskys?" Willing her knees to support her, her pounding heart to behave, she lurched free and headed back into the house. "Maybe I should sleep in the bathroom with the door bolted against any further amorous attempts." Her words held all the sarcasm she could muster.

"Jesus!" He swung away from her, and she heard him drop back into his chair.

Chapter Thirteen

"Ross, breakfast!" Jessi ladled out a plate of bacon and eggs and called down the hall. No response. A scowl marring his features when she'd first come into the kitchen that morning, he'd muttered he was going out on the verandah to drink his coffee. Her repudiation of the previous evening apparently was still eating at him.

When he didn't respond, she went to find him. The verandah was deserted, but movement out on the water caught her eye. Ross?

He'd gone swimming! Alone! She took off at a run toward the beach. If he drowned, Laura would never, never forgive her.

His clothes lay in a heap at on the beach. *Skinny dipping like a teenager. Good God, what is wrong with the man?*

"Ross, come in here…now!" she yelled, glad there was no wind to carry her words away. The bay lay in a dead calm, something for which she was grateful. At least no waves would overcome him.

"Hello," he shouted back, that infamous grin creasing his face. He began to tread water. "I decided to take a dip. Why don't you join me? The water's great."

"I'm not into skinny dipping, thank you very much," she snapped, giving the pile of his clothes a kick with her toe.

"Too bad. It can be great fun…in pairs. Didn't you tell me I once caught your eye when I went swimming with my brother out at your family's ranch?"

"Stop dredging up history. I was a curious kid back then."

She turned away and started back toward the farmhouse.

"Wait!" he called after her. Then, more softly, "I think I overdid the swimming bit. I'll probably have a rough time getting back to the house. I wouldn't mind a little help."

The words, his first admittance of vulnerability, made her stop short and swing back to face him.

"Of course…" she began, then whirled away. He'd stood up in water that barely covered his hips and was wading toward shore. "Oh, for God's sake, Ross!"

"It's usually the gentleman who turns discreetly away to allow the lady to maintain her modesty," he said, a taunting tease in his voice as she listened to him wade to shore.

"That's because real gentlemen don't parade around naked where a lady might see them."

"Oh." He sounded contritely amused as she heard him shaking out his clothes. "I wouldn't faint or feel compromised if you did take a peek. But"—he sighed—"you've missed the opportunity. You can turn around now."

Slowly, suspiciously, she turned to find him wearing his jeans. Dark hair glinting with water drops in the sunlight, broad chest and shoulders rippling with muscles above a narrow waist and flat belly, Ross Turner took her breath away.

He paused a moment, then bent awkwardly to pick

up his shirt and cane. He stumbled and appeared about to fall. Jessi rushed to his side. And, just as fast, he caught her into his arms.

"Jess," he breathed, blue eyes warm, caring, and sensual all at once. As he lowered his head to kiss her, she felt again the same wild, heady rush of sensations she'd experienced the night before on the verandah. She'd attributed most to the night's sensuous ambience, but this was nine in the morning, for God's sake!

"What am I going to do about you?" He drew away, looked deeply into her eyes. "You're starting to scare the beejeebers out of me."

"Scare?" Jessi stared up at him. *I'm drowning in blue, pools of blue.*

"I could get in way too deep with you. My mother knew what she was doing when she chose you to come down here. You're not just a pretty face and a great body, Jessi Wallace. You're a real three-alarmer to someone like me."

"Someone like you?"

"Someone who's always managed to avoid serious commitment; someone who used to think all he needed to make him happy was another rodeo and another championship."

"And you're afraid I might muck up all those carefully cultivated ideas?"

"Possibly." He caught her hand in his and brought it palm upward to his lips in a gesture so erotic her breath hiccupped in her throat.

"So." He drew it down to his side and exhaled. "We'll have to take it slow and easy from here on."

"We'll! We'll?" She jerked herself free and glared up at him. "I think the correct pronoun is 'you'll.' If you've been paying any sort of attention to our relationship, any and all advances have been at your instigation. And to top if all off, you go skinny dipping!"

"Damn it, woman, sometimes I think there's no pleasing you. First you force me to swim. Now you're in a major snit because I do."

"Not alone, you idiot!"

She turned and stalked off toward the house.

"Hey, you can't leave me now," he called after her. "I could need more help."

"You managed to make it back to the house alone the last time you went swimming. I suggest you do it again," she shouted as she ran up the steps to the porch.

****

"Hey, Jessi, Ross!"

"What...?" At the summons from the front lawn, Ross started to get up from his chair at the kitchen table where he was finishing his breakfast. Jessi was already headed for the verandah.

When he caught up with her, she was greeting Jake and Shelby, who were mounted on a pair of fine-looking horses. Shelby had two more saddled animals in tow, while Jake led their daughter's pony with the child clad in helmet and padded riding jacket on its back.

"We finally got a morning clear of commitments and thought you might like to come for a short ride with us." Jake was grinning as he jerked his head over the word "short" toward his daughter.

"We'd love to." Jessi accepted the invitation before Ross had a chance to speak. "Gorgeous morning for it. Just wait until I put on my boots and get a hat." Giving

Ross a smug glance, she brushed past him as she hurried into the house.

"What's your pleasure, Ross?" Jake indicated the two lead horses, one the pretty sorrel mare he remembered from the corral, the other the big white gelding he recalled had been another of its occupants.

"The gelding looks fit. I'll get a hat. I'm already shod for the event."

Moments later, Stetson in place, he put his left foot in the stirrup, drew a deep breath, and swung aboard, gritting his teeth to ignore the pain the effort caused.

"Ready?" Shelby asked, turning to look at him and at Jessi already mounted on the sorrel mare.

"Ready and rearin' to go." Jessi grinned.

"Rearin' to go." Katie Rose squinted up at her father in the sunlight. "Come on, Daddy. Move it."

"Move it?" Shelby turned to frown at Jake.

"She spends a lot of time with Grady." Jake winked at Ross. "Must be picking up some of his language."

Ross's mouth twitched into a grin. It felt good, better than good, to be back in a saddle. These friendly down-home-type people added to the pleasure.

"We usually ride up the shore below the cliffs beyond here," Shelby said as the group headed toward the beach. "Lovely scenery."

"Sounds perfect." Jessi brought the sorrel mare up beside the vet's while the men fell into place behind them.

"How about a canter, Jessi?" Shelby had been holding Fancy to a prance. "This girl has been cooped up all week and is ready to run."

"Sure."

"Jake, get a hand on Midnight Brandy," Shelby called back to her husband. "You know his race-horse mentality."

"Sure, sure. Hang on a minute." Her husband handed the pony's reins to Ross. "I'll need both hands to keep this black devil under control."

"Not a problem." Ross grinned down at the child. "Silver and Pretty are probably good friends, right, Katie Rose?"

The child nodded as her father spoke to her mother. "Okay, Shel, I'm braced. Go for it."

As the two women took off at a gallop, the big black gelding snorted, shook his head, and pawed the sand.

"Whoa, whoa," Jake managed a smooth, soothing voice as he swung the animal around to bring him out of sight of the racing mares. As the women vanished around a bend in the shoreline, the animal quieted, and his rider turned him back to face up the beach.

"Good handling," Ross complimented him.

"Yes, well, maybe. Five years ago, he threw me flat on my backside the first time I tried to ride him."

"Brandy threw Daddy on his backside." Katie Rose chuckled.

"No need to repeat that to Mommy, baby." Jake winked at Ross. "Now let's go. Can't let those women leave us too far in the dust."

They started at a walk up the beach. Ross, still holding the pony's lead rope, sucked in a deep breath of the sea-spiced air. Damn, it felt good to be back on a horse, enjoying a fine morning in the saddle.

"Great place, isn't it?" Grinning over at him, Jake broke into his thoughts as the meadows that stretched down to the shore gradually gave way to rising cliffs that stood out thirty feet above them.

"Sure is."

"The first year I worked for Shelby, there was a motor vehicle accident at the top of that cliff over there." Jake pointed to a sharp promontory ahead of them. "Horse trailer rolled, and a mare spilled out and down the bank."

"Was she killed?"

"No, just scared to death and cut up a bit. Shelby got the paramedics to lower her down to the shore, where she finally managed to settle the animal, and we eventually were able to lead her to a place down near your farm, beyond the cliffs."

"We?" Ross was quick to catch the change of pronoun.

"I got lowered down to help her."

"Good for you, man. I'm guessing that back then you didn't have a lot of horse savvy?"

"Definitely not. Do you know, the first time I tried to put a bridle on Candy, I only got one ear through the strap? And I didn't like to tighten a girth because I was afraid of hurting her. Great old girl, that Candy. Tolerated me no end."

"But you managed."

"Yes, I managed, but at that time, going out for a ride like this today would have scared the beejeebers out of me. Now, thanks to my wife, it's pure pleasure."

"You couldn't ride before you came here?" Ross looked over at him, surprised.

"Definitely not. But Shel is one great teacher...and doctor. When I arrived here, my gut was so screwed up I was well on my way to serious ulcer troubles. She saved me from a major health issue. She's one amazing woman."

He paused to look over at Ross before continuing more slowly, "And unless I'm a really poor judge of character, you've got the same kind of lady in Jessi."

"I don't have Jessi." The words broke out more harshly than he'd intended, and he hurried to make amends. "Sorry. Didn't mean to snap. It's just that Jess and I have been shoved together by my well-meaning mother. She thinks Jess can cure me the way she cures horses. In the process, I'm pretty sure she's also hoping Jess will fall for her gimpy-legged son. It's not going to happen." Ready to change the subject, he turned to the child on the pony. "How about a little speed, Katie Rose?"

"Go, go!" The little girl's face lit up. "Go, Uncle Ross."

"Uncle?" Ross glanced at Jake.

"She wanted to know what to call you and Jessi, so we told her 'uncle' and 'aunt.' Hope you don't mind. Mr. and Miss seemed a bit formal."

"Don't mind a bit." *Uncle Ross. Yeah. I like it.*

Ross felt a warm sense of belonging as he urged the gelding to a quick walk. The child squealed with delight when the pony broke into a slow, shambling trot to keep pace.

"No need to tell your mom, though," he cautioned.

Jake winked and nodded.

Ahead, Shelby and Jessi came back into view as they rounded a bend in the shoreline. They were coming at a dead run, apparently racing.

Midnight Brandy snorted, half reared, and began to prance, tearing up the sand.

"Whoa, whoa." Jake kept his voice low, soft, and calming, but the excited animal backed and whirled, slamming into Pretty. The pony shrieked as a hoof hit her rump and projected her into the water.

Later, Ross wouldn't be quite sure how he managed it. All he remembered was his heels banging Silver's sides. The big albino leaped forward, in time to allow Ross to scoop the child from the frightened pony's back before she could be tossed into the bay.

Only once the little girl was clutched in the saddle in front of him, did he realize what he'd done. Suddenly he was surrounded by Jessi, Shelby, and Jake, who'd dismounted and were holding their horses' reins. Midnight Brandy still snorted and pawed, but Jake had the situation under control.

"Oh, God!" Shelby's face had paled under its tan. "Oh, God! Thank you, Ross, thank you." She held up her arms for her child.

"Fun." Grinning, Katie Rose looked down at her mother. "Uncle Ross, wasn't that fun?" She turned against his chest to look up at him with delighted blue eyes.

"Yeah, yeah, fun." *Good God, am I shaking? I hope she can't hear my heart pounding.*

"Katie Rose, come." Shelby was still holding up her arms for the child.

"No." She settled herself into the saddle. "I want to ride home on Silver with Uncle Ross."

"Katie Rose…" Shelby began to protest, but Ross heard himself stopping her.

"It's fine, Shelby. I'll take her home…or at least as far as my farm."

"Shel, I think that would be a good idea." Jake

joined the discussion. "She's had an experience, and Ross stepped in to settle it. She'll feel better with him."

"Okay." Doubt coloring her tone, Shelby caught up Fancy's reins. "Katie Rose, be good for Ross."

"Mommy, look!" The child pointed to her pony standing by the water's edge. "Pretty is bleeding! Brandy kicked her!"

"Oh, God..." The exclamation was a mutter from Shelby as she handed her reins to Jake and strode across the sand toward the little animal.

"Is Pretty going to die, Daddy?" Wide, frightened blue eyes looked down at her father.

"No, of course not, baby. Your mom's the best vet in the world, we both know that, right?"

"Right...I guess." A frown puckering her face, Katie Rose watched her mother examining the pony.

"Just a cut. Pretty will be fine." She turned back to her daughter and smiled. Taking up the pony's reins, she walked back to join the group.

"Good." In his arms, Ross felt the child heave a sigh of relief. "Let's go, Uncle Ross."

"Uncle?" Jessi turned a quizzical look up at him.

"Yeah." Ross gave a smirk. "While you were off racing, Katie Rose gave me the title. Oh, and by the way, you're now Aunt Jessi."

"So let's go, Uncle Ross." The child bounced impatiently. "I want to go fast. Can you make Silver run?"

"Probably." Ross fought to quell the shakes. "But I don't think your parents would approve."

"Okay." The word came out slowly, tinged with disappointment.

"Nerves of steel...just like her mother," Ross heard

Jake mutter as he remounted Midnight Brandy. He looked over at Ross. "I'm never sure if that's good or bad."

"Come on, Uncle Ross." Katie Rose wiggled in the saddle. "Let's get the show on the road."

"Jake, we really have to speak to Grady about how he talks in front of her." Shelby spoke to her husband.

"Yes, definitely."

The group started off, Ross leading the way with the little girl.

"Let me have the reins, Uncle Ross." She looked up at him with those resolve-melting sapphire eyes. "I know how to steer."

"Not just yet." A contented feeling settled over him as he kept his arms around her, holding Silver to a sedate walk. "You still have a lot to learn. Jumping ahead too fast isn't a good idea."

"I suppose." She sighed. "But you'll teach me, won't you, Uncle Ross?" She glanced up at him again. "Mommy and Daddy and Grady are so busy all the time…"

"We'll see what your parents think."

Apparently satisfied with his answer, she settled comfortably into the saddle in front of him.

A sudden, unexpected thought enveloped him. What would it be like to have his own child riding with him, asking him to teach her to ride, giving him those cute grins?

Where in hell did that come from? I'm not the father type. I'm not Chase.

But the thought didn't leave as easily as he'd imagined. He glanced over at Jessi. She smiled.

****

152

"Look, a bunny!" As they arrived on the beach in front of the Turner Farm, Katie Rose pointed at the small, brown animal sitting up on its haunches in the overgrown lawn a few feet away. "Let me down, Uncle Ross, let me down!" She began to squirm.

"Go ahead." When Ross shot a questioning glance at the child's father, Jake responded with a resigned grin. "You won't get any peace until you do. And I'm pretty sure the rabbit is in no danger of capture."

Ross dismounted and reached up for the little girl. She slid from the saddle into his arms and gave him a quick hug.

"Thanks for the ride, Uncle Ross." She planted a kiss on his cheek before wriggling in his grip. "Put me down, please. I have to catch that bunny."

He placed her on the ground, and she darted off after the rabbit. The little animal bounded off toward the house with Katie Rose in pursuit.

"Sorry I didn't control Brandy better back there, Shel." Jake took the opportunity to apologize to his wife as the rest of the riders dismounted.

"No, it was my fault." Shelby touched his arm. "I know better than to do anything that even remotely resembles racing within his sight. It was just that it was such fun to have an all-out gallop with someone who…"

"Can ride well enough to keep pace with you?" Jake grinned and put his arm around her shoulders. "Don't be afraid to say it. I wasn't born to the saddle like you and your brother. I know I'll never be able to give you competition…on a horse."

"Jake!" She gave him a light punch in the shoulder.

"Look." Jessi laughed. The rabbit had vanished

under the verandah. Katie Rose's bottom stuck out as she tried to continue her pursuit.

"Oh, Jake, go get her before she gets herself stuck and we have to dismantle Ross's front steps to rescue her."

"Wouldn't make much difference," Ross remarked as Jake set off. "A few more bits broken off won't make it much worse."

"Can you come in for coffee…or a beer?" Jessi invited. "Not sure what the rule is about offering a guest alcohol before riding home on horseback, but if it's permitted in New Brunswick…"

"I don't think there are any Royal Canadian Mounted Police waiting along the shore to check our alcohol consumption level, but we should be heading home." Shelby glanced at Pretty's shoulder. "Contrary to what I told Katie Rose about the pony being fine, I really need to get antiseptic on that wound. Another time?"

"Definitely."

Jake returned with the little girl by the hand, her face contorted with discontent.

"But, Daddy, if you'd just let me wiggle a bit more, I could have caught him."

"Yes, and maybe broken some boards on Uncle Ross's steps. You wouldn't want either him or Aunt Jessi to fall because you'd made a hole, would you?"

"No-oo, but I was this close to his tail." She held her fingers a couple of inches apart.

"Come on, enough rabbit talk." Shelby swung onto Fancy and held out her arms. "Up you come, Great Bunny Hunter. Jake, I'll lead Silver and Brandy. You can ride Candy and lead Pretty."

"Back in the beginners' circle." Jake cast a rueful glance at Ross and Jessi. "How ignominious."

"Stop feeling sorry for yourself and enjoy an easy trip home." Shelby turned the horses up the beach. "Wave good-bye, Katie Rose."

"Bye, Uncle Ross, Aunt Jessi. Come see me soon."

Chapter Fourteen

"Hello." Jessi answered Ross's cell. He'd left it lying on the counter while he went outside to check the gas gauge in his truck.

"Good morning…or afternoon…whatever in the hell time it is there." The male voice was gruff but not unfriendly. "Ross around? It's Simon Shoeman."

What does he want? Jessi recognized the name of one of Alberta's most prominent rodeo organizers. Suspicious, she fought down the impulse to say Ross wasn't available, but knowing the man's reputation, she knew he wouldn't give up until he'd accomplished whatever he was after.

"He's in the yard. If you'll hold, I'll get him for you."

"'Preciate it."

Carrying the phone, Jessi walked out onto the veranda and handed it to Ross as he came up the steps.

"It's for you. Simon Shoeman."

Ross's eyes narrowed as he squinted up at her in the sunlight, his features hardening as he took the phone.

"Simon?" His tone was neither friendly nor welcoming. "What's up?"

Jessi turned away and headed back into the house. Ross should be left to handle the call in privacy.

Once inside, she couldn't resist peeking out a

window. Ross was limping back and forth on the lawn, still talking into the phone, his scowl indicating his attitude hadn't mellowed.

When Ross took the phone away from his ear, he punched off hard and fast. As he headed toward the house, she scuttled into the kitchen, opened a cupboard door, and pretended to be perusing its contents. When he stepped inside, she turned innocently toward him.

"An old friend?" she asked.

"Don't play dumb. Anyone around the rodeo circuit knows who Simon Shoeman is," he snapped, dropping the phone onto the table. "And you can make a damned good guess at what he wanted me for." He hobbled to the sink, took a glass from the cupboard beside it, and turned on the tap. He filled it and took a long drink.

"Why don't you tell me?"

"He wanted to know when I'd be ready for the circuit…rodeos south of the border this winter."

"Oh." Jessi quietly closed the cupboard door and waited for him to continue.

"Is that all you've got to say?" Annoyance filled his voice as he turned off the tap. "Isn't this where you're supposed to become my mother's advocate and warn, beg, threaten, or cajole me into staying put?"

"Would any of those tactics work?"

"No."

"Okay, so I'd be wasting my breath. Consequently, you can stop huffing and puffing. You don't have to blow over any buildings to convince me."

"You have to be the most irritating woman I've ever met!"

"That translates as persistent." She put her hands

on her hips and grinned at him. "Thank you. I've always been proud of that quality."

"Ah, man!" He headed for the front door. The abrupt squeal from the porch swing told her he'd flung himself into it.

Jessi smiled. Later she could tell Laura that as least for the immediate future Ross wasn't planning to return to work.

****

"Sure, be glad to help." Jessi punched End on her phone and turned to face Ross as he sat slouched in a chair at the kitchen table the following morning. "Shelby needs someone to watch the farm for a few hours this afternoon. She has to take Katie Rose to the pediatrician, Jake is busy at the school, and Grady has to deliver a mare to a client. I said we'd be glad to."

"Nothing serious wrong with the little girl? I didn't hurt her when I pulled her off that pony, did I?" The thought jolted him alert.

"No, nothing like that. Just a regular checkup." Jessi returned to putting their breakfast dishes into the dishwasher. "We have nothing pressing to do, so we may as well farm-sit."

"No need for us both to go." An idea forming in his mind, Ross stood and went to get another cup of coffee. "I think I'm capable of sitting alone on their porch steps for a few hours and keeping rustlers at bay."

"Now you're being a smart-ass." Shelby closed the door of the machine with a bump. "But okay. If you feel you need a few hours away from me, fine. Give Fox a hug for me."

She poured herself another cup of coffee, and sauntered toward the front of the house. "I'm going down to the beach to enjoy this great morning."

Damn, this is going better than I'd hoped. Not a single word of protest. He grabbed his cane and followed her, a sly grin quirking one corner of his mouth.

****

"Grady has all the barn work done." Shelby hoisted Katie Rose into her safety seat of their king-cab truck. "You might check on Fox once in a while, but try to keep her quiet. Now are you sure you'll be okay watching the place?"

"I'm pretty sure." Ross leaned on his cane and watched as Shelby fastened her daughter in place. "I don't expect I'll have to fend off too many rustlers in this quiet place."

"You wouldn't think so, but several years back, someone stole Midnight Black."

Shelby climbed into the driver's seat and fastened her seatbelt.

"You're putting me on. Around here?"

"Not here on the farm but at a show we were attending. Luckily we got him back unharmed."

"Must have been an experienced wrangler to get that big guy to go along with him."

"It was a woman." Shelby turned the key in the ignition. "Long story. There's fresh coffee in the pot and lots of cookies in the jar on the counter. Enjoy. Oh, by the way"—she paused as she reached to shift into drive—"you can take Fox home when you leave."

"Great! See you." Ross stepped back and waved as Shelby turned the truck toward the road.

He watched until they were out of sight, then turned to the house.

First, a visit to Fox. Poor little bugger. Left with a probable permanent limp. Well, at least she has three other good legs and won't have to use a cane.

****

"Easy, big guy." Ross stopped outside Midnight Black's steel-barred stall and spoke softly.

The stallion snorted, half reared, then settled down to pawing at a horse toy the shape and size of a large beachball.

"How about a little music?" Remembering the calming result of Grady's snapping on the old CD player, Ross pushed a button. As an old Jordan Brooks hit filled the air, Midnight Black paused, gave his head a final shake, then settled, apparently listening.

How about that. Never seen the likes. But if it works...

He reached for a saddle blanket on a sawhorse against the stall and eased open the latch on the door.

"Now, big fella, let's see if I've still got anything near what it takes to ride a bull."

****

Holding the stallion's lead rope in one hand, the CD player in the other, Ross limped carefully into the arena. His cane hung from the saddle. Slowly, so as not to stop the flow of music, he placed the machine on a ledge inside the door and fastened a lunge line to the big black's halter.

"Go." He removed the cane from the saddle horn, leaned it against the wall, and took a long whip from a wall hook. Stepping away from the horse, he loosened the lunge line and raised the whip to shoulder level. It was a gesture only. A trainer never touched an animal with more than the lightest of taps when lunging it.

Black shook his head, pawed for a moment, then took off at a lope in a wide circle around the man.

"Good, you know the drill. Get all that wild energy out before you take me for a ride."

He let the big animal gallop, then trot, and finally slow to a walk. When the horse came to a standstill, blowing and shaking his head, Ross decided it was time to give it a go.

Getting his injured left leg into the stirrup took more than a bit of forbearance. When he put as much weight on his right as possible in an effort to save the injured one as he swung into the saddle, he gritted his teeth. Midnight Black shifted under the awkward mounting.

"Easy, fella." Ross stifled his discomfort as he settled into the saddle, and the horse, responding to the words and hands of an experienced rider, quieted.

Damn, but this feels great.

Ross squared his shoulders and looked around the arena with all the pride of a cowboy heading out on the range on a beautiful Alberta morning.

"Now, Mr. Black." He spoke to the horse as he turned the animal's head to start around the perimeter. "Let's take us a little walk."

****

They'd circled the arena a number of times, first at a walk, then a trot, and finally a lope that, in spite of pains jerking up his leg, Ross recognized as smooth as a rocking chair.

A great animal to use as a stud. And with the music, as rideable as anything I've ever handled.

Then it happened. The CD player hiccupped, played a couple more ragged bits, and stopped.

Midnight Black skidded to a halt. For a moment, he stood stock still, ears twitching. Silence. With an outraged snort, he reared.

Years of experience coming to the fore, Ross managed to keep his seat. But when Black bucked and sunfished, he lost it. His weak left leg couldn't withstand the jolt of twelve hundred pounds of angry horse twisting and hitting the ground under him.

He flew through the air and landed hard on the arena floor, his right shoulder taking the brunt of the blow.

Then, nothing.

****

"Who the hell are you? And what are you doing with our horse in our arena?"

Ross opened his eyes to see a good-looking young man with dark hair squatting beside him, his expression a mixture of concern and annoyance.

"Tryin' to ride that big black bugger over there." As his head cleared, he managed to pull himself up on one elbow and grimaced toward Black, now standing placidly beside the CD player once more spouting music.

"Why? And who gave you permission to do such a crazy thing?"

"I'm farm-sitting for Shelby and Jake."

"Farm-sitting? Where's my sister and her husband…and my niece and Grady?"

Questions flew from the new arrival. Ross's shaken mind slowly began to take in the words and give them sense.

"You're Shelby's brother?"

"Right. Hey, man, maybe I should call 911. You're

looking more than a bit grim."

"No!" He grabbed the younger man's arm as he pulled a cell from the pocket of his plaid shirt. "No." He softened his tone as his companion stared at him, astonishment in his gaze. "I'm fine. I don't want anyone else to know about this." He rubbed a hand on his throbbing thigh. "I'm pretty damned sure neither Shelby nor Jake would take kindly to what I tried, never mind Grady. And I've got a lady at home who thinks she's my nursemaid. I'd get one hell of a lecture from her."

"Yeah, well…"

"Hey, rude of me." Ross stuck out his hand and all but cried out as pain ripped though his shoulder. "Here I am asking favors and I haven't introduced myself. Ross Turner. I live over at the old Turner place."

"Travis Masters." He hesitated only a moment before accepting Ross's hand.

"Travis Masters the singer?" Ross stared as recognition dawned. "Hell, this is an honor. You got some great tunes."

"Thanks. Need a hand up?" He stood.

"No…maybe…yeah." Ross gave up the struggle to right himself. "Maybe you could get my cane. I left it against the wall over there."

"Sure." Travis gave him a puzzled look before heading off.

"Here." He handed the cane to Ross.

Damn, it hurt, but he grasped the stick and staggered to his feet.

"Mind if I ask why you decided to tackle a horse like the Black when you're…"

"Crippled? Don't be afraid to say it. I'm getting

used to it. Trying to prove myself. Stupid, right?"

"Stupid, maybe, but understandable. Say, didn't I see you last summer at the Stampede in Calgary?" Travis furrowed his forehead in thought. "Yeah, now I remember. Hell, you're *the* Ross Turner, bull riding champion. I thought I recognized you."

"Once upon a time." Pain surging through his right shoulder, Ross fought to carry on a polite conversation. "What brings you back here? I read somewhere that you were on a world tour."

"I'm home for a few days before me and my band head off to Europe. Sure will miss this place." He turned to let his gaze roam around the area, finally ending up on the stallion enjoying music in the corner. "Hope I get back for Christmas."

"It is pretty fine." Ross forced a grin and stifled the urge to vomit. *Hell, I did give myself a royal smash. Better get on the road back home before this fella decides he really should call 911.* "Well, now that you're here to keep an eye on things, I'll be off…just as soon as I unsaddle that black devil and rub him down."

"I'll take care of the Black." Travis put hands on hips encased in tailored jeans. "I think you should head home for a good stiff drink and a hot shower."

"Sounds like a plan. Sure you don't mind?"

"It'll be great to spend time with the Black again." He grinned. "Go on. Or am I supposed to pay you for farm-sitting?"

"Forgetting what you just saw will be more than enough compensation."

"Consider it forgotten."

"Good. I'll just get my dog from the surgery and head home. Tell Shelby I'll be by tomorrow to square up with her." He paused. "Give my back a brush off, will you? No need to sport evidence of my stupidity."

****

"Ross, I'm making barbecued chicken in the oven for supper...oh, my God!"

Jessi had stepped into the parlor to find Ross, fresh from a shower, struggling to get his right arm into a shirt. "What happened to your shoulder?"

A black-and-blue bruise covered half of his back.

"Nothing, nothing." He forced his arm into the sleeve, his face twisting. "I banged myself on the truck door." Fox sat beside him. Her tail hadn't stopped wagging since he'd bundled her into his truck for the drive home.

"Really?" She went to adjust the shirt over his shoulders, the word reeking of sarcasm.

"Well, not exactly." He began to push buttons through holes with what she recognized as an effort.

"Here, let me." She rounded on him and took over the task. "Supper will be ready in about a half hour."

"What? No inquisition? No demand for details?"

"Look, Ross, I know you well enough to realize pestering you right now for details will get me nowhere. I'm going back to the kitchen to get an ice pack. Sometime, some day when you feel like it, you can tell me the truth."

She started out of the room but turned back. "You didn't break anything, did you? Bull riders are pretty good at diagnosing broken bones."

"No, no breaks."

"Good." She fought to hide her concern, which she knew wouldn't be welcome. "Glad for that. I'd hate to have to leave supper half-cooked and rush you off to

165

the hospital."

"Aren't you going to offer me any further comfort? A shot of whisky…a massage?" The last reeked of smug sexual innuendo.

"Do you want a shot of whisky and a massage?" She wasn't about to let him get the best of her.

"No." He sank into a chair by the unlit fireplace. "But a beer would be nice…along with that ice pack."

"Beer and ice pack coming up."

Back in the kitchen, as she checked the chicken and made an ice pack, she puzzled over this latest injury. It must have happened at Ebony M Farm, but how? Had one of the horses charged him? She didn't believe Shelby and Jake kept any renegades…except maybe their stud. Shelby had told her the stallion they called Midnight Black could be difficult if a person didn't understand his whims.

She paused, an ice cube tray in hand. Oh, God, no! He couldn't have been so crazy! He couldn't have thought riding a stud stallion with a whole lot of quirks would be a way to prove himself. The tray dropped onto the counter, and she stared out the window, remembering Simon Shoeman's call.

It added up. His shoulder bore witness to the fact that he'd most likely been thrown, and thrown hard. Outrage fountained inside her. Where was the man's common sense? Was he so eager to get back to rodeoing he was willing to risk his life to do it?

She cracked ice into a plastic bag, an urge to hit him over his stupid head with it enveloping her. Maybe she'd throw that beer in his face, as well. Anything to bring him back to sanity.

Fuming, she got two long necks from the fridge,

removed the caps, and took a long swallow from one. Didn't the man have a single ounce of common sense? She sucked in a deep breath and ordered herself to keep a cool head. By the time she returned to the parlor, she believed she had a firm hand on her emotions.

"Feels good?" She sat down opposite him as he applied the ice pack to his shoulder.

"Yeah." He took a pull on his beer and leaned back in the chair with a flinch.

"Better than getting tossed on your backside by Shelby and Jake's stud?" She let the words come out matter-of-fact.

"Who told you?" The words snapped in an accusation as he jerked upright and grimaced.

"Guessed. Simon Shoeman's call, your being all by your lonesome over at the farm…not hard to put those two events in logical order."

"You'll be really happy to learn I found out I'm not ready to go back on the circuit. I imagine you'll be making a secret phone call to my mother to give her the good news."

"I hardly think telling her you were crazy enough to attempt to ride a half-wild stud stallion will cheer her up."

"Midnight Black isn't half-wild. In fact, he's about the smoothest ride I've ever had…on a horse." She knew the sly, suggestive smirking words were meant to disarm her.

"Really? Then you haven't had as much experience as I credited you with."

"Argh!"

Her cell rang, and she pulled it from her pocket.

"Shelby? What? Slow down—I can't understand.

Katie Rose is missing?" She listened. "When? How? Of course we'll come. We're on our way."

Chapter Fifteen

Jessi punched End and stared at Ross, shock holding her in its grip.

"What? What is it? Did you say Katie Rose is missing?" He was on his feet, inches in front of her, staring down into her face.

"Yes. I don't have any details. Shelby was too upset to talk. Supper will have to wait. Let's go."

By the time she'd turned off the stove and shoved the chicken into the refrigerator, Ross was in his truck and revving the motor, Fox sitting in the back seat. She barely had time to jump into the passenger seat and buckle up before Ross spun the vehicle out of the yard.

As he drove down the rutted road, his face tense as he stared ahead, he said, "Give me what details you managed to get."

"Just that Katie Rose is missing. We'll have to wait until we get to Ebony M and talk to Shelby."

"She might just have wandered off somewhere on the farm." Ross's jaw working with a nervous tick belied the words.

"Let's hope so. Let's hope by the time we get there she's been found."

****

"Jessi, Ross! Thank God you've come!" Dr. Shelby Masters-Brooks, normally calm in any crisis, met them at the barn, her face the color of death. "I can't find her anywhere! I've called Jake. He's on his way home from school. I couldn't reach Travis. He's visiting friends and probably has his phone turned off. He does that when he wants to avoid his agent. Oh, dear God, where can she be?"

"Suppose you start by giving us some details." Ross appeared cool, but Jessi knew him too well not to sense the tension behind his quiet demeanor.

"I came home to find my brother taking care of the place. Apparently you'd been called home." Jessi cast Ross a knowing look, but he ignored her. "He said he wanted to visit a couple of friends before supper, so I told him to go. He'd just left when I heard a horse in distress in the barn. I knew one of our customer's mares was about to foal, so I told Katie to stay outside the barn while I checked on her.

"It turned out the animal was in trouble, and I had to help her. I'm not sure how long it took, but just as the foal was getting to its hooves, I heard a vehicle barrel into the yard. It stopped for a minute, then took off again. I got to the barn door just in time to see a black van racing toward the road. And Katie Rose was nowhere in sight. Oh, God!" She clutched both sides of her head and moaned.

"Did you get a license number, a make of vehicle, anything?" Ross was asking the appropriate, police-like questions.

"No license number, a Ford or Chev, I think."

"Okay." Ross pulled out his cell. "911, here we come."

****

"I'm going crazy, Jessi." Shelby paced her living room, rubbing her temples. "I can't just sit here doing nothing…I can't!"

"It's what the RCMP told you to do…in case she wanders home." Jessi, seated in a chair by the fire, struggled to find words to calm her friend.

"Or in case there's a ransom demand, or they find her… Oh, God, Jessi, if we lose her…"

"You won't. Jake and your brother are out patrolling the roads with the RCMP, there's been a Canada-wide alert issued for that van, and every neighbor in the area is helping. Come, sit down. You're wearing yourself out."

"More coffee, ladies?" Ross came to the living room doorway. He'd been manning the phone. He and Jessi had made Shelby see the wisdom of having someone besides herself fielding calls.

"Thanks, Ross, but I'm already jumping out of my skin." Shelby drew a deep breath. "And it's getting dark." She glanced toward the window. "Oh, God, it's getting dark!"

As Jessi went to put a comforting hand on her friend's arm, Ross jerked his head in the direction of the kitchen.

"I'll be right back, Shelby," she said. "Ross wants to speak to me."

"There hasn't been a phone call…something you haven't told me?" Shelby's voice rose sharply.

"No, no." Ross was quick to reassure her. "I just need to speak to Jess for a minute."

Once in the kitchen, he turned to her. "I have an idea. It's a long shot, so I don't want to raise any false hopes in Shelby. I'm going to saddle Silver and take Fox out around the barn. Maybe the dog can pick up a scent." He took a small pink jacket from a peg near the door. "I'll let Fox sniff this and hope she's got a bit of tracking sense. For all we know, Katie Rose may just have wandered off into the woods behind the barn."

"But the van…?"

"May have been nothing more than someone looking for a vet in a hurry. When they thought the place looked deserted, they drove off fast to find one somewhere else. Tell Shelby I've gone out to tend the stock."

****

Fox hobbled ahead of him, nose to the ground, as he kept Silver to a sedate walk behind her.

"I hope you've got a good nose, girl, and that you're not just smelling out rabbits."

As he watched her hobbling in front of the horse, he couldn't help admiring her determination. Bandages still around her shoulder, her front right leg all but useless, she nevertheless was willing to try to do what Ross expected of her. Whether or not she'd understood when he'd thrust the pink jacket to her nose, only time would tell.

She had run in circles just outside the barn door before starting off sniffing left and right down the trail into the woods. Among the trees, darkness had fallen. Long shadows reached out across the trail in front of them.

If she's out here, she must be scared to death. Come on, Fox, find her.

As if sensing his silent plea, the little dog stopped and tilted her head to one side.

"Do you hear something, girl?" Ross held Silver quiet and listened.

Nothing.

He decided to take a chance.

"Katie Rose, where are you?" he shouted. "It's Uncle Ross. I have Silver. I'll give you a ride home."

This time he heard it. A muffled cry that sounded like his name.

Fox apparently heard it as well. She stumbled into the trees beside the trail and down a ravine a few feet beyond.

Heart banging at his ribs, Ross dismounted and followed. "Katie Rose," he bellowed.

"Uncle Ross, Uncle Ross."

Knees weakening with relief, he followed the sound. Moments later, he found her curled up against the trunk of a pine, Fox eagerly licking her face.

"Katie Rose!" He dropped on one knee as she stumbled to her feet. Then she was in his arms and he was holding her, crushing her to his chest.

"Uncle Ross, you're squeezing me too much." She struggled in his grip.

"Sorry, honey, sorry." He lessened his hold and bundled her into his arms to stand. "Are you hurt?"

"I skinned my knees when I fell." She snuggled against him as he began to struggle up the side of the ravine. "I almost caught that blasted bunny. Then I went ass over appetite down the bank."

A grin tugged at Ross's mouth. More of Grady's lingo. He didn't care. Let her parents correct her. Right now he just thanked God she was in his arms and not in the back of some infamous black van.

****

"We're home." Ross opened the farmhouse door with an awkward move that made the child in his arms giggle. Fox hobbled in beside them and fell down on the floor.

"Don't drop me, Uncle Ross."

"Never, baby, never."

"Oh, dear God, Katie Rose!" Shelby burst out from the living room. For a moment she stared at the pair. Then she rushed forward to gather the child into her arms. Tears streamed down her cheeks. "Katie, Katie, Katie!" She crushed her against her.

"Mommy, you're squeezing too much...just like Uncle Ross when he found me."

She put a hand on each side of Shelby's face and grinned at her. "Mommy, don't cry. I'm fine. I just chased a bunny."

She glanced at Ross, and he gave her a thumbs up. *No "blasted" or "ass over appetite." The kid knows her boundaries.*

"Ross, where...how...?" Shelby stared at him over the child's head.

"We'll get it straightened out later. Right now"—he looked at Jessi, who'd come to stand in the door that led to the parlor—"we'd better get on the horn and call off the search. I think her dad and her uncle will be glad to get the news."

"I'm on it." Jessi pulled out her cell and began punching in numbers.

"Mommy, I need a bath." Katie Rose held up dirty hands. Her face was streaked with dirt, and the knees of her jeans torn.

"Of course you do, sweetheart." Shelby started for the stairs but paused to turn back.

"Ross, thank you. A thousand million thank-yous."

"No problem."

"Search successfully terminated." Jessi punched in

more numbers as mother and daughter disappeared in the direction of the stairs. "Now to let her father and uncle know."

"Hello, Jake. Jessi here. Ross found Katie Rose. She chased a rabbit into the woods and got lost. Yes, yes, she's fine. Shelby's giving her a bath. Yes, I will thank Ross. See you soon." When she'd finished her call, Jessi came over to stand close in front of him.

"Looks like you're a definite hero, Ross Turner." She stood on tiptoes and kissed him. "I think you deserve a beer. I'm sure Shelby and Jake won't mind if you help yourself to one from the fridge."

"In a minute." He knelt beside Fox, lying on her side, tongue lolling out of her mouth where she had dropped on entering the kitchen. "This little girl needs water, just a bit. Too much wouldn't be good for right now. And when she's rested, food. She found Katie, not me."

"Good girl." Jessi dropped down beside the pair. Then, "Ross, look. There's blood coming through her bandage!"

"Jesus!" He stared at the red circle near the dog's shoulder. "She's torn her stitches."

"She's bleeding." Jessi examined the bandage. "The stain's getting bigger, but we'll have to wait until Shelby gets Katie Rose to bed before we can trouble her with this problem."

"Yeah, yeah." Ross dropped his hand on the dog's head. "Easy, girl, easy. You did a great job tonight. We'll get you fixed up real soon."

But a chunk of something hard and cold had settled in his chest. She was panting hard, her eyes glazing over. He knew the signs.

****

They were both still on the floor with the dog when Jake and Travis burst into the kitchen.

"Where is she?" The words jerked from Jake. His face was a mask of tension.

"Upstairs having a warm bath." Jessi looked up at him.

He strode across the kitchen but paused at the door to turn back, hand extended down to Ross. "Thanks isn't near enough to express how I feel right now, Ross." The emotion in his eyes all but undid Ross.

"Glad to have been able to help."

"We'll talk later. Right now, I have to see my baby."

"Sure." And Jake was gone, bounding up the stairs in strides they could hear.

"I'll let him have his reunion with his kid and wife." Travis pulled off his jacket and hung it on a peg by the door. "What's wrong with the dog?"

"She was recovering from a car accident." Ross stroked her head as her eyes closed. "I thought she might be able to track the little girl, and she did. But it was too much for her in her condition. She's opened her wound." He pointed to the slowly widening circle of blood. "We're waiting until Shelby gets Katie Rose to bed…"

"I don't like the looks of this." Travis got down beside them. "It should be taken care of right away."

"We can't expect Shelby…" Jessi began.

"No, but you can expect me." Travis drew a deep breath. "I used to assist Shel in the surgery before I went on the road and Jake took over. If you'll trust me, I'll see what I can do." He looked up at Ross.

"Sure."

"Okay. I'll get a blanket, and we'll carry her into the surgery. Jessi, Shelby told me you have experience with injured horses. I'll need an assistant. How about it?"

"I've never actually done surgery, but if you think I can help, sure."

****

Ross was sitting in the parlor, nursing a beer, when Jake came back downstairs.

"How is she?" Ross stood too quickly and flinched.

"Bathed and fast asleep in her bed, holding onto that ragged pony." He sucked in a deep breath. "How can we ever thank you, Ross?"

"Ah, lucky guess, nothing more."

"Nevertheless, your finding her means the world to Shelby and me. Someday, when you're a father, you'll get the full impact of what you did for us. Come into the kitchen. I'm going to make Shelby my mother's cure for bad times...hot, sweet tea."

Ross followed him, the words about his being a father someday resonating in his head. Except for that fleeting moment on the beach the day he'd pulled Katie Rose to safety, he'd never considered fatherhood. He'd planned on letting Chase be responsible for producing the next generation of Turners.

"Where's Jessi and Travis...and Fox?" Jake asked as he held an electric kettle under the tap.

"Jessi and Travis are in the surgery." He took a swallow of beer before he continued. "Fox's wound opened. They're stitching it up."

"No!" Jake turned off the tap and turned to him, the word echoing his distressed surprise. "Shelby told me

177

the little dog tracked Katie Rose and found her. Damn it, don't tell me she's in danger now."

"Fox'll be okay." Ross sat down at the table and watched his thumb run up and down the bottle's surface. "Your brother-in-law said he's had lots of experience assisting Shelby, and Jess has a big reputation for healing...horses."

"Hell!" Jake plugged in the kettle and went to the refrigerator for a beer. He slumped into a chair opposite Ross. "What a night!"

"Yeah."

****

Ross vaulted to his feet as Jessi and Travis came back into the kitchen. He couldn't bring himself to ask the question.

"Looks good." Travis, wearing scrubs, put his hands on his hips and drew a deep breath. "I'm pretty sure she'll be okay, but I'll have Shelby take a look at her when she's available."

"Can I see her?" Ross rubbed sweaty palms on the seat of his jeans and wet dry lips.

"We put her on the back seat of your truck," Jessi answered. "We'd better be going, Ross. She needs to be settled to rest, and bumping over that trail to the farm won't do her much good." She began to pull off the scrubs covering her jeans and shirt.

"Right. Good, very good." Ross realized he sounded rambling but he didn't care. Fox had a chance. He held out his hand to Travis. "Thank you, my man."

"Don't thank me just yet." He grinned the grin that drove young women worldwide crazy and made men try to emulate. "I've been out of practice for a while. Where's Jake and Shelby and the kid?"

"Upstairs. Asleep, I'm guessing. They had a tough night."

"Definitely." Travis began to remove his surgical clothing. "Guess I'll follow them. Thanks again, guys."

****

They drove in silence until they entered the lane to the farmhouse, and then Jessi spoke.

"What a terrible experience for Jake and Shelby…and Travis. I can't imagine anything worse than losing a child."

"You got that right." She looked over at him, at the hard planes of his handsome face as he concentrated on easing the truck over ruts and roots.

"Ross, what's wrong? You've been silent as the grave since we left Ebony M Farm. Fox is going to be okay, I'm sure of it. Travis did a great…"

"Damn it, Jess, it's not Fox…well, partly, I guess, but it's more. Something Jake said…about me understanding how he and Shelby felt when I had kids of my own."

"He was right. Only a parent can truly experience the emotions they suffered tonight."

"Yeah, well, Jake got me thinking. I don't want that kind of gut wrenching, not now, not ever. I'm willing, more than willing, to leave all that to Chase."

"But maybe now you can start to appreciate how your parents felt when you got hurt, when they didn't know if you'd survive." The words burst out, and immediately she knew they were exactly the wrong ones in the circumstance.

"Ah, God!" He hit the gas and the truck jumped over an exposed root. "Here we go again. The old psychology bit."

"Ross…"

"Jesus, Jess, can't you give it a rest? Guilt trips never work with me."

"Oh, fine, sure." His lack of empathy suddenly rankled her to the bone. She let loose with all the vehemence she'd been containing. "Hide from anything that lets anyone see the great Ross Turner can be vulnerable, can actually care for anyone beyond himself. Go back to Alberta and ride bulls until you get killed or permanently crippled. Let your brother carry your family's future entirely on his shoulders. Why should you care? You've got crowds to please, buckle bunnies to satisfy!"

"You got that right, and I'm sure as hell not ready to leave all that behind to settle down with a wife and kids who'll drive me crazy."

"What? Where did that come from?"

"Oh, come on. You don't really think I swallowed all that crap about your coming down here to save me from myself out of any idea of repaying my family for helping yours out, did you?"

"Okay, then you tell me. Why did I come?"

"To find yourself another washed-up rodeo cowboy willing to marry you and settle down to life on your father's ranch…to replace Clint Harrison."

"Are you crazy? After Clint Harrison, what would make you think in your wildest thoughts that I'd be looking for another tomcat cowboy?"

"By trying to show me how great life is for Shelby and Jake. Well, that backfired big time tonight, didn't it? There's no way I want that kind of responsibility."

He slammed on the brakes, jolting her forward. They'd reached the farmyard, and the lights of the truck pointed out onto a bay still and blank in a deadly calm. He swung out of the truck and opened the rear door. A moment later he'd gathered Fox into his arms and was walking toward the house with long, uneven angry strides.

"Wait!" Jessi jumped out and ran to get ahead of him. "Wait," she continued more softly as she caught up to him on the verandah. "Let me make a bed for her beside your mattress."

His reply was a grunt as she opened the door and held it for him.

"Thanks." The word was half mutter, half grunt as he moved past her.

Chapter Sixteen

Once Fox was on blankets beside Ross's mattress and appeared settled to sleep, Jessi headed for the bathroom, pajamas in hand. Animosity still thick between them, he hadn't spoken since his curt "thanks" at the door. Trying to get more words from him could only result in a further confrontation, Jessi realized. At the moment she felt too weary to spar with him.

When she returned to the parlor, he was gone, but Fox had been covered with a light blanket, which she hadn't been when Jessi had gone to shower.

The man does have a heart, but it's buried deep, deep.

But where was he? Surely he hadn't gone swimming again. For a moment, fear gripped her. She went to the front door and opened it. A soft snore from the direction of the old hammock at the far end brought a small grin of relief to her lips. Moving softly, she went to look at him, sprawled in the swing.

Exhausted. And more emotionally than physically ...even though he'd be the last person on earth to admit it.

She returned to the parlor and picked up a blanket. As quietly as possible, she went back onto the porch and covered him. He moved and muttered but didn't wake.

Content she'd done all she could for him, she went

back inside and checked on Fox. The little dog opened her eyes at her touch, then returned to sleep.

Jessi lay down on her mattress and tried to settle to rest. It didn't come easily. Ross had accused her of trying to trick him into marriage, of making him a substitute for Clint Harrison. As if! Was the man crazy?

****

She woke to the smell of coffee. For a moment she lay still, getting her thoughts in order, thinking back to the previous day...the evening and night in particular. What an emotional roller coaster it had been. But, she thought as she sat up and rubbed sleep from her eyes, it had all ended well...sort of. She added the last as she remembered the angry words she and Ross had shared. Hopefully, in morning light, they could put it behind them and start again. It had been an emotionally charged night.

She got up and went into the bathroom to brush her teeth and hair. She almost continued on to the kitchen in her pajamas before she remembered Ross's remark about this not being a frat house.

When she arrived in the kitchen a few minutes later, she wore jeans and a sweatshirt that read "Product of Alberta."

"Good morning." She decided to pretend those angry words hadn't passed between them hours earlier. Fox, who'd been lying at Ross's feet beneath the table, struggled up and staggered to greet her. "Looks like a fine day. Fox seems on the mend." Bending to pet the dog, she glanced toward the window.

The answer was a grunt.

"So it's going to be like that, is it?" In spite of her resolve to let bygones be bygones, his reply brought it all back.

Who does he think he is? What gives him the right to stay emotionally outside the box of living?

He stood and went to replenish his coffee.

"Oh, God, Ross, don't act like a disgruntled twelve-year-old. So you got tangled up yesterday in a whole bunch of feelings you didn't know you had. So you found out Ross Turner could actually be afraid. So what! Everyone is afraid at one time or another. Discovering you're no exception isn't a disgrace."

"Yeah, well, maybe being expected to be a platonic roommate with a female horse doctor who was sent, against my wishes, to work her magic on me is really grating on me. I didn't sign up for any of this nonsense, as you'll recall, and now I've had enough!"

He shot her a look that would have curdled milk, then headed toward the front of the house. The slamming of the front door marked his going out onto the porch.

****

The sound of a vehicle gunning up the drive late that afternoon drew her attention to the kitchen window. A black convertible braked to a stop, its wax job so intense that, combined with the sun glinting off the windshield, for a moment Jessi couldn't make out the driver.

"Ross, where are you, sweetie?"

A tall, willowy brunette stepped out, waist-length hair so black it gleamed blue-black. She wore jeans that might have been painted on, and a black leather jacket. Knee-high boots completed the appearance of sexy and knowing it.

"Ross!" Apparently spotting him on the front

verandah, the woman strode around to the front of the house. "God, I've missed you, baby."

Was this the infamous Catherine Holt, the woman Laura Turner wanted her to keep away from Ross? An intense desire to make the uninvited woman as unwelcome as possible engulfed Jessi She'd be justified, wouldn't she? After all, hadn't Ross's mother deputized her to keep the woman away from her son?

She stepped out onto the verandah to find the woman with her arms around Ross's neck, kissing him.

"I see you're not alone." She stepped back and jerked her head in Jessi's direction. "I might have guessed. I should have known there was more to this recluse thing than you were telling Simon." She surveyed Jessi critically. "Cute." The word was cold and demeaning. "Introduce us, sweetie."

"Okay." Ross stepped aside and turned to be at a right angle between the two women. "Catherine, meet Jessi Wallace. Jess, this is my…friend, Catherine Holt."

"Call me Cat." The woman advanced toward Jessi, a slender hand tipped with long nails painted crimson extended. "Ross does."

She ended with a sly half-smile that narrowed her eyes as she looked over at him.

"I had no idea Ross was expecting a visitor," Jessi replied, her insides quivering like an injured child's lower lip. *Play it cool, girl, play it super cool. More flies with honey than vinegar, remember.* "I was preparing dinner. Will you join us? I'm sure you and Ross have a lot of catching up to do."

"She cooks, too." Cat withdrew her cool hand from Jessi's and turned back to Ross. "You really lucked out this time, sweetie."

"Jessi's pretty remarkable in a lot of ways." Ross squinted up at the two women on the doorstep. The sun shafting through the trees was catching him directly in the eyes. "But you probably don't have time to stay…"

A sense of satisfaction washed over Jessi. Ross was squirming…invisibly, but nevertheless squirming. A smug sense of satisfaction settled over her.

"Now, there you're wrong, sweetie." Catherine Holt swung back to him. "Thank you for the invitation, Jessi. I've already booked a dinner reservation for Ross and me at what I've been told is your little town's best restaurant, but it will only take a second to cancel it."

"Cat, I don't think…" Ross glanced at Jessi.

"Wonderful." Jessi fought to make her words sound carefree and welcoming.

"Come on, baby." Cat slid an arm around Ross's shoulder, and Jessi felt a perverse sense of satisfaction as he flinched. *She won't be getting much lovemaking out of that banged-up cowboy tonight.*

But remember, a nagging little voice reminded her, *he's been celibate a very long time, and that woman is sex on the hoof. And he is a rodeo cowboy.*

"Yeah, well…" He took one more backward glance at Jessi.

"Come on, sweetie." Cat had taken his hand and was drawing him toward the house. "Let's see what you can scare up in the way of a before-dinner drink. As I recall, you used to make a wild mix of whisky and…what was it?"

"Yeah, well, we don't have much of a bar here. You might have to settle for a cold beer."

"Fortunately, I came equipped." She released him and trotted back to her vehicle. She reached inside and pulled out a bag with a liquor store logo.

"Ta-da!" She held it up. "Twelve-year-old Scotch and a choice bottle of dinner wine." Returning to Ross's side, she drew him past Jessi, murmuring just loud enough for her to overhear, "Remember what happened the last time we drank dozen-year-old stuff, cowboy?"

Ross shot Jessi a furtive glance before they went into the house together.

"Argh!" It was Jessi's turn to snarl…silently.

****

"I must say, Jess, I didn't expect anything nearly as tasty as this." Catherine laid aside her napkin and picked up her wine glass to twirl the red liquid inside. She raised her drink. "My compliments to the chef."

"Hardly anything exotic." Jessi stood and began to remove the dishes. "Just lasagna from the freezer, and a Caesar salad. Maybe it was the wine that made it more palatable. I'm nowhere near a connoisseur, but I'm guessing it's an excellent vintage."

"Nothing's too good for my baby." She smirked over at Ross.

Shut up, Cat. Just shut up with the "baby" stuff. Ross wet his lips and wondered how long it would be before his deodorant gave out. Although both women were behaving civilly, he could feel animosity bubbling just below the surface. And yet, why on Jess's part? She'd made it clear she wasn't about to get involved with him, had vehemently denied having any designs either on him or his future.

"Dessert?" Jessi had stacked the dinner plates and stood with them in her hands. "I have blueberry pie fresh from the Carleton Bakery."

"No, thanks, sweetie." Catherine finished her wine

and stood. "Some of us take care of our figures. Come on, Ross. Let's head into this little town to see what night life it has to offer. I'd ask you to come along, Jess, but I'm sure you have a sick horse somewhere that needs tending. Never fear, I'll take good care of this stallion."

"Cat, I don't think…" Ross got to his feet, trying not to flinch as pain darted through his shoulder.

"I won't be asking you to think, baby." She pulled on his hand. "If we can't find any night life, we'll retire to my room with the whisky. I know how well you can perform after a few shots, no thinking required."

"Go ahead." Jessi was looking at him with green eyes as cold as emeralds encased in ice as Cat's persistence dragged him to his feet. "I wouldn't want either of you to miss out on that kind of fun evening."

"You're a sport, Jess." Catherine smirked.

As Cat linked her arm into his and urged him toward the door, an image of a stallion being led out to cover a mare slashed across his mind. Bloody hell, he was better than that.

"Go on out, Cat." He wrenched free with a force that made him grit his teeth, but he had to talk to Jess…alone. "I need to…freshen up."

God, where did that girly excuse come from?

"Fine, but if you're heading back to your room to pick up protection, don't worry, I came prepared." She sauntered out, hips swaying. "Don't keep me waiting too long, baby."

"Jess." He turned to her after the door had closed behind Cat. "You have to understand…she and I have a history…but it's just that…history."

"No need to explain." She turned her back, rigidly

straight, to him, and crossed her arms. "No doubt some recreational sex will do you good."

"Recreational…? Jesus, Jess, is that what you think of me?"

"You're a rodeo cowboy, aren't you?" She swung on him. "You're all about as faithful as tomcats, I've learned from past experience. So go. Get drunk on expensive whisky and have an all-night party with Cat, *baby*… I couldn't care less!" She turned and strode down the hallway to the front of the house. Fox, after giving him a baleful glance, followed.

Aw, hell, now even my dog hates me.

He headed for the door. Maybe a night with Cat and a bottle of Scotch was just what he needed.

Thunder rumbled as he crossed the verandah and headed down the steps.

Another damned storm is rolling in. Perfect!

****

Ross sat in the suite Cat had rented at the hotel in Carleton and nursed the drink she'd mixed for him.

God, what was in this stuff? *A couple of sips and I can feel it*. He set it aside.

He rolled his shoulders and grimaced. His right one hurt like hell. Attempting to ride Midnight Black had been a damned fool thing to do, but he'd had to try to prove himself.

But he hadn't, had he? He looked around the fancy suite and wondered if this wasn't what he was trying to do again…prove he was man enough to go back to his former lifestyle in all its components, including this kind of careless sex. What if he failed here, too? He'd felt no overwhelming sexual desire for Cat…not like he once might have…not like he'd felt for Jessi when he'd kissed her. No, definitely not like he'd felt for Jessi…

He stood and picked up his Stetson just as Cat came out of the bedroom wearing a bit of black lace that left little to the imagination, a glass half full of whisky in one hand.

"Ready, cowboy?" She struck a seductive pose.

"Sorry, Cat, this isn't going to be any good for me." He slapped his hat on his head. "It's not you…"

"Oh, good God! Don't even say, 'It's me.' I couldn't bear that crummy old line."

"Well, then I won't."

He headed for the door, but she rushed to get between him and it. With her back to it, she faced him.

"If you really meant what you said…that bit about it not being me but you…does that mean you're not 'up' to it anymore, that the accident did damage that doesn't meet the eye?"

"Let's just say the accident changed me." He moved her gently aside. "You can tell Simon Shoeman whatever you like, if it will save your dignity."

"Changed you? I'll say it did!" She flipped the glass upward, flinging the contents over his face and shirt front. "Damn you to hell and back, Ross Turner!"

"Don't ever do that again." The words were a growl so fierce she backed off a couple of steps, empty glass in hand.

Wiping his jaw with the back of one hand, he pulled open the door and started down the corridor. She stepped out of the room and yelled, "It's that little cowgirl you're shacked up with, isn't it? She must be one hot piece, to make you walk away from me!"

Two young men emerging from the elevator at the end of the corridor, stopped to stare.

"Lovers' scrap," Ross explained with a rueful grin as he walked past them.

"Ah, man, and you're walking away from all that?" One of them pointed at Cat standing hands on her hips in the revealing negligee.

"Yeah." He pushed the Down button. "Sometimes it's just the right thing to do."

Chapter Seventeen

"Hello." Jessi's tone registered her distraction as she answered her phone an hour after Ross had left.

"Jessi? Is everything all right. You sound strange. Is it Ross? Is he…?" Laura Turner's voice quickly filled with concern.

"No, nothing's wrong…not really. Ross's fine. He's walking without his cane, actually."

"Then why the 'not really'? Jessi, I can tell when you've got concerns." Laura Turner's tone relaxed only slightly. "Talk to me, young lady."

"Cat Holt showed up here this evening." Jessi's reply was a breath of weary exasperation. "She and Ross have gone out on a…date."

"Cat? In Carleton? I was hoping I'd never again hear her name—which, by the way, fits. Jessi, you have to put a stop to that, get rid of her. She'll try to convince Ross to go back on the circuit. She'll ruin his life!"

"Laura, I'm aware that you had hopes for us, but knowing what you do about Clint and me, you must have realized how unlikely they were. Ross isn't interested in anything permanent…including me."

"And what about you, Jessi?"

"After Clint Harrison, I've had my fill of rodeo cowboys…even ones like your son."

****

Rain lashing his windshield, Ross drove through Carleton and out to the shore road that led to his farm, only to find it barricaded by police.

"Sorry, sir," the officer informed him. "We had to shut it down. Waves are going over the road in several places."

"So when are you anticipating it will be open again?" Suddenly Ross couldn't wait to get back to Jessi.

"Not before morning, and even then only after the department of transportation has had an opportunity to assess the damage."

Ross turned his truck and started back into town. He'd have to spend the night, but where? He sure as hell wasn't going back to that hotel where Cat might well still be in a major snit. Walmart. That was it. Walmart allowed RVs to spend the night in their parking lot. He didn't imagine they'd object to one king-cab truck.

He glanced at his watch. The store might still be open. He'd buy a sleeping bag and pillow and try to get a half-decent night's sleep in the back seat before he faced the problems he foresaw back at the farm. Then another thought struck him.

Damn it, they may not serve me, smellin' like drunk of the year. They may even call the cops to report someone they suspect of drinking and driving. Well, I'll have to chance it. If the police do come, I'll let them breathalyze me.

****

The storm clouds that had started to roll in off the bay shortly after Ross and Cat left blotted the sky with a mottled charcoal cover. The wind rose and howled about the farmhouse. Jessi cleaned the kitchen and went into the parlor with a cup of coffee. She ignored the uncomfortable old sofa and curled, with her back against the wall, on her mattress. She'd lighted a fire on the hearth, but now she decided it would be best to allow it to burn down because of the wind howling down the chimney. No telling when the old stone structure had last been cleaned. A chimney fire on such a night could be disastrous.

Fox climbed up and rested her head in her lap with a sigh.

"He left with that witch." She stroked the little dog. "We had a fight, and he left with that beautiful, sexy witch." She paused, then continued, "But why should I care? I'm a veteran of two-timing cowboys." Another pause. Then: "What am I saying? Two-timing? In what universe would Ross's taking off with an old girlfriend in any way be two-timing me? There's nothing between us…except a couple of stellar kisses and…maybe a few hot fantasies…and maybe some warm, cozy ones," she concluded, thinking back to the domestic contentment she'd witnessed between Jake, Shelby, and their daughter.

Fox looked up at her and whined.

"I know, I know. He's been good to you. I guess he does have some good points. Still, going off with a woman called Cat! Unbelievable."

But, a nagging little internal voice muttered, *he has been celibate since the accident. Maybe even for a while previous. And he has respected you even though you're sleeping in the same room.*

The wind shrieked to new heights of violence. The electric lights flickered twice, three times, and went out.

"Lovely." She moved Fox aside and got up to light the lanterns on the mantel. "Glad you're here, girl. This promises to be the proverbial dark and stormy night."

****

Late the following afternoon, Ross drove into the farmyard. He was glad he'd insisted on taking his own truck the previous evening, following Cat into Carleton instead of relying on her for transportation. But then, he knew her. She'd left him stranded on more than one occasion. The question now was what kind of a greeting was he about to get inside the old house.

Fox burst from the back door, barking her joy at seeing him. *Well, at least one female is glad I'm back safe and sound.*

He got out and headed for the house, limping even though he no longer had to. *Maybe a little sympathy might rear its head?*

"'Afternoon." He stepped into the kitchen, spoke, then froze. Jessi stood by the table dressed in a short tangerine-colored dress that clung to every curve of her body, a single wide strap over one shoulder holding it in place. Cut down to there and up to there, the outfit made his breath catch in this throat. The woman inside it caused his gut to do a double take. Jessi Wallace hair piled on her head, a few errant curls caressing creamy cheeks, slender gold earrings moving when she turned her head to face him—was a total knockout.

"What's all this?" He struggled to subdue Fox's exuberance and get himself re-centered.

"I've got a date." She leaned against the cupboard and crossed her arms.

"With who? You don't know any men around here except Grady and Jake, and I'm pretty damned sure neither of them…"

"I don't see as how it's any of your concern." Green eyes, hard and bitter, narrowed as they looked over at him. "You appear to have had quite a hot date last night yourself. You reek of stale booze and look as if you'd been hit by a bus."

"Hot date! What are you talking about?"

"Don't pretend you and Cat Holt didn't rekindle the old fires."

She was angry, angrier than he'd ever seen her, than he'd ever suspected she could get.

So she does care. Now I just have to get out of this hole I've dug myself into.

"Jess, listen…"

The sound of a vehicle coming up the lane stopped him. *Jesus, don't let it be Cat. Not now.*

"That will be *my* date." She swept a cream-colored shawl from the back of a chair and swung it about her shoulders. "Fox has been fed, and there's a fire laid in the parlor. All you have to do is drop a match into it. Cold chicken in the fridge."

"Now just a damn minute!" By this time he was getting angry. He wasn't about to let her walk out with another man with things the way they were between them. He followed her as she went out the back door. "I have a few things to say…"

His words trailed off as Clint Harrison stepped out of a gleaming red sports car.

Aw, hell and damnation! Not that bastard!

"'Evenin', Ross." The bronc rider grinned as he strode around the vehicle to hold the passenger door open for Jessi. "Takin' my girl out for dinner. Don't bother to wait up."

He winked, and Ross felt his hands knotting into fists at his sides.

Nothing he could do. He'd screwed up big time, and Jess had made a choice. He could only watch as the bastard gunned that fancy car around, tearing up chunks of dooryard, and headed back down the lane way too fast, a hand out the window waving at him.

****

He stood and went to the window, the beer still clutched in his hand. The sunset across the bay was a mixture of pinks and oranges beginning to purple as night began to arrive. He wished Jessi were there beside him to enjoy it. He wished he could take her in his arms and tell her how special she'd become to him, how he'd never met anyone like her, how…

"Argh!" He broke off his thoughts and finished his beer in a long, single drink. What was the use of wishing for what wasn't going to happen? Obviously she still had feelings for Clint Harrison or she wouldn't have gone out with him. Clint Harrison with two good legs. Clint Harrison who hadn't been stupid enough to go off with an old flame that meant nothing to him.

Well, he could still feed himself and put himself to bed. And that was exactly how she'd find him when she got home…fed and asleep.

****

"Kind of surprised you agreed to come out with me so easy." Clint lowered his wine glass and looked over at her in the candlelight of the upscale restaurant to which he'd taken her. He was working his way through a second bottle. "You ignored my texts and phone calls all summer. Comin' down here was a last-ditch effort on my part."

"Really? What made you decide to come now? Rodeo season slowing down, or is your butt getting too sore to go on?" She narrowed her eyes and looked over at him.

"Come on, Jess. You know it's how I make a livin'. I couldn't just up and leave mid-season."

"Not even for two or three days? You could have caught a couple of red-eyes here and back…just to see how I was doing."

"And what would I have been seein', Jess? You and that has-been bastard of a bull rider gettin' it on?"

"Hold it right there, Clint. Ross and I are simply friends…good friends. As you'll remember, you were the one snuzzling up to Ginny Morgan. By the way, don't you think you've had enough?" She gestured at his glass.

He started a reply, a nasty one if Jessi knew facial expressions and body language. Then he paused, drew a deep breath, and let a slow, sly grin move over his face.

"This snipin' at each other won't get us anywhere, honey." Jessi could see and feel him working to turn on what he considered the full force of his cowboy charm. "Hell, woman, I didn't travel all the way out east with Cat Holt just to do battle with you."

"Cat Holt? You came to New Brunswick *with* Cat Holt?"

"Yeah, well, sort of. Damn it, must be the wine. That was a stupid slip."

"How do you 'sort of' travel with a woman? Is she your latest…what I'm too much of a lady to say?"

"No, no, nothin' like that."

"Then what? You and that woman arriving here at the same time does seem a little too coincidental."

"It's like this. I was goin' into Simon Shoeman's office to check out some schedulin' when I caught the tail end of his phone conversation with Ross. By the time he'd hung up, I had a plan. I'd offer to come down here to see how Ross was doin'."

"And of course Simon would pay your way."

"Not at first. He said he knew about you and me and how you were with Ross now. He didn't seem to think I was a good candidate for the job. Then his eyes kind of lit up, and he said Cat Holt would do just fine. If anyone could get Ross back on the circuit, she could."

"So how did you manage to come along with her?"

"I did a bit of fancy talkin', convinced him that Ross would never come back if he was all snuggly with you here in New Brunswick, but once I arrived, you'd leave him in a cloud of dust."

"Always so cocksure of yourself, aren't you, Clint!" Flinging her napkin onto her plate, Jessi jumped to her feet. "Just watch me leave *you* in a cloud of dust."

She snatched up her shawl and strode out of the restaurant. Clint started to follow, only to be stopped by the cashier.

"Your cheque, sir?" Jessi heard his pursuit halted.

****

"Where can I get a taxi?" Jessi stopped a couple about to enter the restaurant.

"One block over." The man pointed. "But if you have a cell…" He gave her a number she punched into her phone as he reeled it off.

Once she'd placed her order, she decided it wouldn't be safe to stay in front of the brightly lighted restaurant. Moving as quickly as she could on her ridiculously high-heeled shoes, she hurried into the shadow of the alley beside the building.

She leaned against the cold brick and held her breath.

"No use tryin' to hide, baby." Clint, his face flushed from wine and anger, appeared around the corner and grabbed her arm. "Walk out on me, will you?" The hard planes of his face had become a mask of fury. "Make me look like a fool back there, is that what you were tryin' to do? Well, let me tell you, Miss High-and-Mighty Jessi Wallace, I've had women far better than you, women who know how to satisfy a man, women…"

"Women with no better taste than to get mixed up with a bastard like you!"

Jessi jerked around to see Ross, his expression every bit as bellicose as Clint's, standing, legs planted shoulder-width apart, a dark silhouette at the alley's entrance, hands clenched into fists at his sides.

"Stalkin' us, were you, Gimpy?" Clint glared at him, eyes glinting with liquor and anger in the shaft of street light penetrating the alley. "Well, I'll show you what I think of that kind of slimy behavior!" .

He released Jessi. His right arm flew back. The next instant she flinched as she heard and saw it connect with Ross's jaw. Ross staggered before retaliating.

"Ross, Clint, no!"

People seemingly out of nowhere appeared at the alley entrance. Someone pulled out a cell phone as blows continued to rain.

Shortly, sirens were wailing toward them.

Jessi leaned back against the wall and closed her eyes. She knew better than to try to stop them before the police arrived.

What am I going to tell Laura Turner?

****

Jessi got out of the cab at the farm and paused at the driver's window to pay.

"Thanks for taking me down the lane," she said. "I know it's not the best road in the country."

"I couldn't leave a lady to walk that mess in fancy shoes, especially this late in the evening." The gray-haired driver grinned up at her. "And this old bus, she's been over worse trails."

"Nevertheless, I'm grateful." She added a generous tip to his fare.

"Now, that's not necessary, miss." He looked down at the money. "I have a daughter about your age, and I sure wouldn't want her walking alone down a dark country road."

"Then use it to buy something for her." Jessi turned away and headed for the house.

The cab driver kept his headlights focused on the back porch until she'd opened the back door and waved to indicate all was well. As he swung his vehicle away, she stepped into the lighted kitchen. Apparently Ross had left a light burning.

Fox greeted her effusively, capering around and around her.

"You're not used to being alone, are you, girl." Jessi pulled off her shoes and dropped down to hug the dog. "Oh, that feels good," she continued as she wiggled her toes. "I don't know how women wear heels to work every day."

For a few moments, she sat on the floor enjoying the dog's enthusiasm. This whole situation was getting too far out of hand. She'd done her best to fulfill her promise to Laura Turner. There was nothing more she could do. The situation was way too complicated for her. Cat and Ross getting back together. Clint showing up. Clint and Ross fighting, getting arrested. She had to go home, back to Alberta and her parents and her horses. Back to a place and time where she'd been happy, where she'd be happy again. She took her cell from her purse and punched in a number.

"Hello, Jake. Hope I didn't wake you. No, no, we're all safe and sound. But I do need to ask a favor. Can you take care of Fox for a while? I'm heading back to Alberta in the morning, and Ross is in jail. Yes, that's right, I said in jail."

After promising to give him details in the morning, Jessi ended the call and sat with her back against the door. There, it was done. She was leaving. Exhausted, she dragged herself to her feet and headed for the bathroom. She needed a hot shower, followed by a shot of Ross's whisky and, hopefully, the oblivion of sleep.

****

"Hope you're real proud of yourself, Turner." Clint Harrison glared across the jail corridor from his cell into Ross's. "Bad enough gettin' arrested for fightin', but spendin' the entire night in this pigsty all because this excuse for a town has only one judge and he won't be back from fishin' until noon today… If there wasn't a bunch of steel bars between us, I'd punch you out again."

"Yeah, right." Ross slumped down onto the bunk where he'd spent the night and glared at his bloody knuckles. *Idiot. Fool. Getting yourself into a mess like this...and all for a woman who doesn't give a damn about you.*

"Clint Harrison." A mountie came into the cell area and went to open the man's cell. "Someone convinced the judge to come in early. Come along. He's waiting in the courtroom."

"Well, now, isn't that too sweet." Clint stepped out as the mountie opened the cell door. "I'll bet there's someone just waitin' to bail me out, too? Pretty little lady with golden-blond hair, name of Wallace?" He raised his eyebrows in question to the officer as Ross rose to his feet, clenched jaw ticking.

"Come along, sir." The corporal wasn't about to indulge in conversation with a man in torn dress pants and dirty shirt, a day's growth of stubble making him look all the more disreputable.

"See ya, Turner." The bronc rider grinned at the man still in a cell. "By the time you get out, me and Jess will be Alberta bound."

As the pair left the cell area with Clint Harrison whistling the tune that matched his words, Ross once more dropped down on his bunk. He slammed his fisted right hand into the palm of his left, then grimaced at the pain it caused.

Jess, leaving with that bum. She deserves so much better.

****

Two hours later, the mountie who'd taken Clint from his cell returned.

"Someone is here to get me out?" Ross stood, hearing the words come out like he was an eager school kid.

Man, I feel dirty and sweaty. I need a shower and clean clothes.

"That's right. A man named Jake Brooks."

"Jake?" Glad as he was to be getting out of jail, he couldn't stop the flicker of disappointment. He'd been hoping Jessi…but she'd already bailed out that bum Clint.

"Oh, and by the way." The mountie's words made Ross stop in the cell doorway. "Clint Harrison's release wasn't financed by any blond lady. The woman had long black hair."

"Thanks, Sergeant." Something in Ross's gut revived. "Good to know."

"It's corporal…yet. No thanks necessary. This is a jail, not a torture chamber. I figured your thinking that man left with someone important to you might be causing you some unnecessary discomfort."

****

"Thanks, Jake." A half hour later Ross paused beside his truck that had been left parked in the restaurant lot and turned to the other man. "The last time I got busted for fighting must have been ten or fifteen years ago…stupid kid stuff."

"I think we all went through those events…part of growing up." Jake grinned at him.

"Yeah, well, I'm a little old for it these days. Won't happen again. Right now I'm heading for the nearest ATM. I owe you big time, and the least I can do is get your money back."

"No need. I didn't pay your bond."

"Then who? Jess? Was it Jess?"

His words lilted. She had cared, only she'd been too stubborn or proud, or maybe a bit of both, to come to the jail and to court herself.

"Jessi is on her way back to Calgary." Jake drew his lips into a grim line. "Sorry, buddy. "She left for Moncton with Grady early this morning. He had to pick up a horse down there. She's flying out on a noon flight."

Something dropped like a stone in his gut. Jess, gone. He didn't have to be psychic to know what that meant. She'd had enough. Even her perceived debt to his mother wasn't enough to keep her with him after all the stupid stunts he'd pulled. And what she must have thought about him and Cat…

"Alone, except for Grady?" It was all he could come up with.

"Alone except for Grady."

"Well, that's something." He pulled open his truck door. "I'll be getting back to the farm and a shower and clean clothes. But I haven't forgotten what you did for me…you and some mysterious money person."

"Hold on a minute, Ross. You don't have to tell me, but I admit I'm curious. What caused all this trouble? You and Jessi seemed to be doing pretty good."

Ross paused to look squarely at the man he considered his friend, a confidant. "Okay, here goes." He told about their fight, about his leaving with Cat, about her throwing whisky over him when he told her he wasn't going to spend the night, about the road closure, about going back to the farm to find her dressed for a date with Clint Harrison, about the fight.

"All pretty damned stupid stuff, right?" he finished and waited for Jake's reaction.

"Not for a man in love."

"Ah, come on, Jake. I'm not ready to go there…at least not yet. And I'd be real grateful if you kept all this to yourself. Now, thanks again. I have to get going."

"Not a problem, my man. See you soon." Jake started off, calling back, "You'll have to come over to pick up your dog. Jessi left her with us."

Chapter Eighteen

Ross plunked the pizza box onto the table in the farmhouse kitchen and sucked in a deep breath. Silence and the shadows of a late autumn afternoon surrounded him. Silence and aloneness. Funny, he hadn't minded when he'd first come here. In fact, he'd welcomed it after all the doctors and all the questions of family and friends. But then Jessi had come, and everything had changed.

He looked at the pile of cleanly laundered towels stacked on the dryer, at the clean countertops and scrubbed sink. Even the worn board floors had been swept.

Hell. Does everything have to remind me of her?

He gave his head a shake and went to the refrigerator for a beer. *It'll be better once I get Fox back. I'll eat, shower, and head over to the Ebony M. Hell, I should be relieved the woman's gone. No more danger of getting trapped by my mother's nefarious little scheme.*

But later, as he moved around the house, showering and putting on clean clothes—clothes she'd laundered—relief wasn't among the emotions he experienced. The tidy bathroom and, most disturbing of all, her bed stripped and with bedding neatly folded on its top, brought an unpleasant tightness across his chest.

Jesus, am I having a heart attack? Hell, no. It's

just indigestion from eating that pizza way too fast. A bit of that pink stuff I bought when I was living here alone and eating God only knows what junk will fix me right up.

A half hour later, he climbed into his truck and headed for the Ebony M to collect Fox.

****

"Uncle Ross!" Katie Rose and Fox burst out of the farmhouse and down the steps as he braked to a stop near the verandah.

"Hey, cowgirl!" He caught her up in his arms as he got out and she reached him. "How's my favorite lady?"

"I don't know." She looked at him with a feigned innocence. "You'll have to ask Aunt Jessi."

"Monkey." He tossed her, squealing, into the air before placing her firmly on the ground. He welcomed Fox's cavorting greeting with a pat. "You're looking fit, Miss Fox."

"She's fine." Katie Rose grasped Ross's hand to lead him into the house, then stopped, gazing at his knuckles with wide-eyed astonishment.

"Uncle Ross, what happened?" She looked up at him.

"Uncle Ross fell down." Jake appeared in the front door, Shelby by his side. "You know how rickety his front steps are."

"They are pretty bad." Ross was relieved to see she was accepting the explanation. "And falling off the porch can hurt. Does it hurt, Uncle Ross? Did Aunt Jessi wash your hands and put stuff on them?"

At a loss for an answer, Ross looked at the couple on the veranda for help.

"Katie Rose, Aunt Jessi was just visiting from Alberta." Shelby came down the steps and walked over to the pair. "She has horses and a father and mother out there. She had to go home to be with them."

"Oh." Katie Rose continued to hold Ross's hand as she looked up at him. "I'm sorry, Uncle Ross. Please don't be lonely. You can come over here anytime, can't he, Mommy?"

"He certainly can." Shelby's gaze met Ross's. The understanding and outright sympathy he saw reflected there went right to his heart. She, her husband, and this imp of a child would keep any feeling of loss he might experience at bay.

It would be enough. It had to be.

****

Jessi woke in her bed at her parents' ranch and for a moment lay staring up at the pine beams overhead. Where was the cracked plaster? Then it all came back in a rush. She was home. This morning there would be no Ross moodily drinking his coffee, no little red dog's exuberant greeting.

She pulled herself out of bed and sighed. She should be glad to be rid of the man and his grumbling, of his thwarting her attempts to bring him back to the land of the living. But she wasn't.

Memories of him scooping Katie Rose from a frightened pony before the child landed in Chaleur Bay, of him kneeling beside an injured dog, of him struggling to swim ashore, of him sporting that silly milk moustache…of his spectacular kisses.

She gave herself a sharp mental shake as she headed into the bathroom and forced herself to remember the way he'd looked and smelled after his night with Cat Holt, of his attempts to rid himself of Jessi Wallace, the woman he saw as part of one of his mother's schemes to get him settled down and off the rodeo circuit.

But as she turned on the water and stepped into the warm spray, she felt her lips twitch upward as she recalled the one-way ticket he'd provided in an attempt to return her to Alberta. First class. Hardly cruel or nasty.

She forced her thoughts back to his night with Cat and later his bar-style fight with Clint Harrison. Oh, yeah, Ross Turner and Clint Harrison had a lot in common. She'd hold that thought...and banish the others...especially those about the earth-shaking kisses and blue eyes of a man who'd saved a stray dog and rescued a little girl...twice...and been nothing but a gentleman even though he was sharing a sort of bedroom with her.

She'd put him out of her mind and concentrate on her work. Her mother had said she'd had a barrage of calls from prospective clients while she was gone. Catching up should be enough to drive that man out of her mind...at least temporarily.

As she pulled on her jeans, her cell rang. Relief flooded over her as she saw Shelby's ID. Good, not Clint.

"Hi, Shelby. What's happening in New Brunswick?"

"Quite a bit, actually...where you and Ross are concerned. Jessi, Jake told me something last night I think you should know. Ross confessed to him that nothing happened between him and Cat Holt that night at the hotel."

"What! Ross told Jake? When, why…?"

A sea of questions flooded from her.

"Just be quiet and listen, my friend. But you must never, never tell anyone I told you."

"If it's supposed to be a secret, how did you get it out of Jake? I'm assuming Ross asked him not to tell anyone."

"Last night was Jake's birthday." Shelby's sly chuckle came over the phone. "We were sharing a lovely bottle of wine after we got Katie Rose to bed, and somehow we got talking romance…ours first…then it segued into yours and Ross's. And Jake made a slip…something about Ross being too proud and bullheaded to tell you he'd made a mistake in going off with Cat. So there." Her voice registered vindication. "He wasn't guilty of anything more than a foolish bit of reaction to a silly argument. So call him, Jessi…just to see how he's doing."

Jessi hesitated. Much as she wanted to be in touch with Ross again, she had her pride, too.

"No, Shelby." She shook her head. "I think we both need more time before we're ready to confess we acted a bit off the radar."

****

"I ain't that lonely yet, no, I ain't that lonely yet."

Ross sat on the veranda listening to the old country tune and figured it was an omen. He'd been waffling about calling Jessi, just to see how she was doing, but the words of the old tune from the ancient radio he'd salvaged from the kitchen cupboard made him pause.

"No, damn it, that's true. I'm not that lonely yet." He looked down at Fox curled up at his feet, her nose under her tail like her namesake would have done. "No, definitely not. I have you and the Brooks family. And I could have had one really hot night with Cat a few weeks back, but…"

He stopped and wondered again at his walking out of the woman's hotel room when she'd come out of the bathroom in a bit of black lace nothing. She'd been beautiful, sexy, and willing. What more could a tomcat of a rodeo cowboy want?

Something more, apparently. Something more.

Fox broke into his thoughts by jumping to her feet with a sharp bark. The next minute she was off and running as fast as her game leg would allow, after a rabbit Ross hadn't noticed in the grass a few yards from the steps.

"Fox, no!" He was on his feet, yelling.

Damn it, that was all he needed—Fox to get hurt again.

But she was gone, into the trees.

There was nothing he could do but wait and hope. He sank back down into the chair. He might not be that lonely yet, but he definitely wasn't happy…or even contented. That much he knew.

A sick feeling was gathering in his stomach a half hour later when a dirty red dog emerged from the woods, stumbling into view, tongue lolling out to full length.

"Fox, come here, you stupid mutt!" Anger-induced relief shot through him and made him shout at the dog.

The little dog paused at the bottom of the steps. For a moment, she stared up at him. Then she limped to the verandah and lay down at the far end.

"Way to go, Turner. Alienate your dog. You're getting real good at driving stuff away."

****

"Hey, guys, how about getting the door?" Ross, his arms full of the biggest orange pumpkin he could find in Carleton, summoned attention outside the farmhouse door.

"Ross, what on earth…?" Shelby responded only to stop short, her eyes widening. "Where did you get that?" She pointed at the pumpkin as Ross entered, Fox darting ahead of him. "What? Why?"

"Uncle Ross, you got it!" Katie Rose scrambled down from her booster seat at the end of the table and rushed to greet him as he placed his prize on the kitchen counter.

"Did you think I wouldn't?" He met her enthusiasm with a grin.

"Ross, what is going on?" Shelby put her hands on her hips and cocked her head to one side. "What have you two been up to?" She let her look include her daughter.

"Uncle Ross was telling me about how he and his brother used to make jack-o'-lanterns for Halloween." Katie Rose, after greeting Fox, hurried to the counter to stroke the pumpkin. "He said he'd show me how to make one if"—she turned round blue eyes on her mother—"I promised not to tell you and Daddy. We wanted to surprise you. Guess that idea's off the table now, though. Come on, Uncle Ross." She swung back from petting the big vegetable. "Let's get to it. Tomorrow is Halloween. No time to waste."

"Katie Rose…" Shelby began to admonish, but Jake was beside her, putting an arm around her waist, kissing her on the temple.

"Don't be a party pooper, Mommy." He grinned.

"I'll clear the supper dishes from the table, and we can get started."

"I can see I'm outnumbered." With a smile and a sigh, Shelby turned away and began to help her husband clear dishes from the table. Then she stopped.

"Ross, have you eaten? There's lots of pot roast left."

"Thanks, but I grabbed something in town. Anyhow, I've been eating here way too often. Time I started cooking for myself…again."

"You know we're only too glad to have you join us. But," she continued softly as Katie and her father removed supper from the table, "you've got to stop spoiling her." She gave him a significant look. "It's time you got started on a family of your own." With a sly look, she turned away to join her husband and daughter in their work.

Shortly, the table was cleared, covered with newspapers, and the pumpkin placed in the middle.

"Now." Katie Rose, once again seated on her booster chair, rubbed her hands together in anticipation. "Let's start cutting up this sucker."

"Katie Rose!" Her mother's words made her look over at her. "Jake, have you spoken to Grady about…?"

"I have, but you know Grady." Her husband grinned ruefully. "Says he keeps forgetting himself."

"Sorry, Mommy." For a moment blue eyes looked contrite, then her *joie de vivre* bounced back. "Come on, Uncle Ross, let's…start."

A half hour later a grinning jack-o'-lantern sat in the midst of its innards on the kitchen table.

"Oh!" Katie clapped her hands and grinned. "It's mag…mag…"

"Magnificent, darling." Shelby smiled.

"But that's not all." Ross snapped shut the knife he'd been using to carve, and stood. "Wait a minute."

He went out to his truck. When he came back, he carried a large, thick candle. Bending over the carved pumpkin, he inserted it into a circle he'd carved deep into the bottom. Jake got the idea and pulled a barbecue lighter from a drawer. As the candle blazed to life, Shelby snapped off the kitchen light. The ludicrously grinning face beamed out at them.

"Oh, it's double mag…mag-nificent!" Katy Rose sucked in such a deep breath her mother patted her on the back to make her exhale. "Oh, Uncle Ross, this will be my best Halloween e-e-ever!"

"And you've had so many." Jake chuckled. "Anyhow, I agree. Your uncle has made this one stand out."

"Tomorrow night we'll put it out on the verandah steps, and everyone will see it for miles and miles and miles." She waved her hands out far apart. "And they'll say, 'Look at the mag…magnificent jack-o'-lantern at the Ebony M. Bet they're having the best Halloween e-ever."

"Quite possibly." Shelby snapped the light back on and went to gather up her daughter, sticky with pumpkin innards, into her arms. "Right now, it's a bath and bed for you."

"Ah, Mommy."

Ross blew out the candle. "We have to save it for tomorrow."

"I guess." The child sighed. "Okay, Mommy, let's get to it."

"Jake." Shelby looked accusingly at her husband.

"I'll talk to Grady again."

After they'd gone upstairs, Jake turned to his friend.

"That's a really nice thing you did for Katie Rose, Ross. My brothers and I made jack-o'-lanterns when we were kids. I guess I just kind of forgot, spending years with teenagers who aren't exactly into the magical spirit of Halloween…unless it's the dark magical spirit." Grinning ruefully, he shook his head.

"You mean working in the high school."

"Yes, that and…more."

He didn't continue, and Ross sensed he didn't want the subject pursued, at least not right then.

"How about a beer?" Jake changed the subject.

"Sure, fine, but first I'm going to clean up this mess I fostered. Once Shelby gets Katie Rose to bed, I'm guessing she'll have had a full day."

"*We'll* clean it up." Jake got a garbage bag. "Pick up your work of art, will you, so that I can pull the newspapers out from under it?"

When the table had been cleared and washed, Jake took two long necks from the refrigerator and handed one to Ross.

"Have a seat." Jake indicated a chair and sat down in one opposite.

"Okay, what's up? From the sound of your voice, I'd guess we're on the verge of a serious discussion."

"What's made you think that?"

"It's the same tone my father uses when he's about to give me lifestyle advice."

"Well, I'm not your father, and I'm not going to give you advice…not really."

"Okay, fire away." Ross slouched back into the

chair. "But don't count on success. I'm a pretty independent guy."

"No kidding?" Jake slanted him a grin, and Ross couldn't help replying in like.

"Yeah."

"Ross, you're recovered." Jake grew serious. "You have been for a while. Now don't get me wrong. We enjoy having you around and appreciate all the work you've been doing, helping around the place. Really appreciate it. But it's time you headed back to Alberta and got your life squared away."

"Meaning?"

"Meaning it's time you came to terms with how you feel about Jessi, about maybe planning a future with her."

"Oh, God, not you, too, Jake? I thought you were my best buddy."

"I am. Otherwise I wouldn't be talking to you like this. Look, Shelby and I have seen you with her, have watched you interact with Katie Rose and our family, and we think you should give serious consideration to making a future with Jessi. You can't go back to riding bulls. Or maybe you can…until you're permanently crippled or killed. You're a good man, Ross Turner. You deserve better."

"So you think I should go back to Alberta and romance Jessi into marrying me?"

"Shelby and I both think." Jake looked over at his friend, and Ross saw he was anticipating his reply.

"You do realize that would be playing right into my mother's plans…something I've never done?"

"Yes, but it's more than that, isn't it? I think you're afraid Jessi is only interested in you as a substitute for

Clint Harrison."

"What! Are you crazy?" Ross quaffed his beer.

"Well, aren't you?"

"No…yeah, well…"

"Jessi Wallace is a fine woman." Jake leaned across the table toward him, sincerity emanating from his eyes and words. "She'd no more trade one cowboy for another on those grounds than she'd whip a horse." He moved to settle back on his chair. "Think about that."

"Yeah, well…you think?"

"I know. And what's more, Shelby knows. Women talk, Ross. Shelby and Jessi, in particular."

"Jess said something? When?"

"I can't give you a date, but sometime after she went back west, sometime during one of the dozens of phone calls she and Shelby make to each other."

"Humph."

"Look, Ross, finish your beer, go home, and think about it. You and Jessi will make one hell of a team. And your kids…"

"Whoa, now, slow down, man. There was some pretty nasty stuff took place between us when we split."

"You're not entirely ugly, and you've got a bit of cowboy charm." Jake grinned over at him. "All I'm saying is give it your best shot."

****

Jessi led Maisy out of the barn into the frosty, gray November morning. The little mare's breath came out in a fog as she walked obediently behind her toward the round pen. She was improving every day, but she still had issues, like a coyote's howl or a loud, unexpected noise.

Pausing at the gate, Jessi rubbed Maisy's nose and told herself to be patient. Anything worth accomplishing took patience. And suddenly Ross Turner was all over her mind...all six foot two, broad shoulders, and blue eyes of him. Patience hadn't worked with him. She remembered the way those blue eyes seemed to look right down into her soul, as if they knew all about her, about what made her tick.

And yet he didn't realize you love him.

Good God, where had that stupid thought come from? After what he'd done with that Cat person, nothing could be further from the truth. She shoved open the gate, led Maisy inside, and started her in wide circles around her at a trot.

I've got to start working harder. That's the best medicine for tomcat cowboy blues.

"Jessi!" Her mother's voice calling made her turn toward the ranch house. Joan Wallace stood in the doorway holding up the cordless phone. "Customer."

She released the horse and went out of the pen, latching the gate behind her.

Five minutes later, when she punched End and went back into the house to return the phone to its charger, her mother stopped her with a question.

"Jessi, what happened between you and Ross down in New Brunswick?" She leaned against the kitchen counter, arms crossed on her chest, and faced her daughter. "I told myself I wouldn't pry, but I can't control the question any longer."

"We had a fight, a stupid fight...over Cat Holt and Clint Harrison...both of whom weren't worth the energy we wasted on them." She fought to keep it simple, to satisfy her mother with the fewest details possible. No matter how angry she'd been at Ross, no matter how acrimoniously they'd parted, she wouldn't bad-mouth him to anyone. He was a friend...if nothing more.

"So that's it? That's all? Jessi..."

"Mom, I know you and the Turners had some idea of Ross and me making a couple, of settling down here to sort of unite the families, but that isn't going to happen."

"But surely you can patch things up, now that that woman and Clint are no longer in the picture?"

"It's more than that. Ross and I could never have a proper marriage. He's said he doesn't want children." She left the kitchen and went back to Maisy.

Let that be enough to satisfy her, now and forever. Discussing Ross is just too painful.

Chapter Nineteen

November. Who'd once said of the month, "No warmth, no light, no cheer"?

Ross rode Midnight Brandy through the deepening twilight along a trail bordered by bare limbed maples and birches and felt as bleak as the encroaching gloom. He'd been riding Silver daily at Ebony Farms since he'd gotten out of jail, determined to get himself back to some semblance of his former self. This week Shelby had decided he was up to riding her brother's sometimes fractious gelding. He liked the challenge the beautiful animal offered…a great ride that kept both him and the horse on their mettle.

But spending all that time at the farm with Shelby, Jake, Grady, and Katie Rose had changed his way of looking at life, revived more than his physical strength. The desire to go back to risking his health and even his life for the cheers of the crowd and another championship had dulled. "Been there, done that" had echoed through his mind on more than one occasion. Watching Jake interact with his family was daily giving him more and more food for thought.

He rode into the stable yard and reined to a sharper stop than he'd intended. Someone was playing a guitar and singing…a man…a man who sounded great and stirred a memory he couldn't quite grasp.

Dismounting, he led Midnight Brandy into the

barn, where lights were already on in the early evening gloom. At the far end, outside the Black's stall, Jake Brooks sat in an old plastic lawn chair, guitar in his arms, strumming and singing.

He stopped and glanced up as Brandy's hooves clopped onto the corridor's cement floor. A sheepish grin crossed his face.

"'Evening." Ross paused by his mount's box stall. "Sounds mighty fine, my man."

"Yes, well, I've pretty much given up country music." He put the guitar aside and leaned it against the wall. "This is just a relaxing relapse. Hey, buddy, you're staring. Don't you know that's rude?" He quirked a corner of his mouth.

"Sorry." Ross led Brandy into his box stall and began to remove saddle and bridle. "I've heard that tune played and sung before, and you did it just like…"

He snapped about and came out of the horse's stall to stare at the man he'd come to know as Jake Brooks. "You're Jordan Brooks! I was at your concert at the Calgary Stampede six years ago. Hell, how stupid can I be! I played your CDs for hours, traveling from one rodeo to another. Jake Brooks! Damn it, of course. But…" He slowed down as the other man nodded, grinning. "You had light brown hair, a lot longer back then."

"And now I'm six years older and a married man with a daughter, living on a farm and teaching at the town high school. Quite a change, right?"

"Quite a change." Ross sucked in a deep breath. "Don't the locals give you a hard time…starry-eyed fans and all that?"

"At first, when I married Shelby, for a little while,

but fame, as they say, is fleeting. They soon took up with the next country singer who caught their fancy. Now I'm just another guy around here."

"Don't you miss it?" Ross went back into Brandy's stall. He came out carrying the saddle, blanket, and bridle. "The crowds, the cheering, the excitement?"

"Maybe a little at first, but I knew I was coming to the end of my performing days." He looked down at his hands.

"Why would you think that?" Ross put the equipment into the tack room and came back to face him. "As I recall, you were on top, six years ago. Damn, I enjoyed that song you had at the top of the charts back then."

"Health reason."

"Health reason? Did you get hurt?"

"I did later, in that car accident Shelby mentioned. But when I first arrived here to learn to ride for a movie role, my gut was a mess. Too many hamburgers and fries after midnight, not enough sleep…the list of killers in that lifestyle goes on and on."

"I get it." Ross took grooming rags and brushes from a box and headed back into Midnight Brandy's stall. "Food on the rodeo circuit isn't exactly gut friendly either."

"Shelby saved my life." Jake strummed his guitar. "I'd gotten carried away with a self-destructive way of life at my age."

"That can happen." Ross rubbed Midnight Brandy down with long, skillful strokes.

"Has it happened to you?"

"Not sure. Let's just say I'm doing a lot of thinking."

"Well, here's something that might speed up the process." Jake came to lean against the stall entrance. "You've always wondered who bailed you out of jail a couple of months ago. It was Jessi."

"Jesus, Jessi!" Ross froze, his hand on the gelding's withers.

"She left a credit card, told me to get you out once she was gone."

"And you didn't decide to tell me until now?" Ross advanced toward the other man, his hand on the brush turning white-knuckled.

"You weren't ready to hear it." Jake straightened up to face him squarely. "And Jessi wouldn't have been ready to listen to you. But now, after you've both had time to cool down, to get more than a little lonesome…"

A hot, furious anger engulfed Ross's gut. "Who made you judge and jury in our relationship?"

"Not just me. Shel and I together. We had a rocky start to our relationship, and we saw a bit of similarity in yours and Jessi's. We had to be apart a while to realize just how much we meant to each other. Now"— he moved out of Ross's way—"I'd suggest that as soon as you finish rubbing down Midnight Brandy, you get out your cell and book a flight to Alberta."

"And just what makes you think this is the right time?" Ross scowled at the man he'd come to regard as a friend.

"Shelby's kept in touch with Jessi." Jake shrugged. "She advised me to talk to you, that now is the time for you to make your move. Listen, man, my wife is a clever woman. Trust her. Make the call."

"I have to think about it."

****

Ross stepped into the farmhouse kitchen to Fox's usual profuse greeting. Responding, he wondered what he'd do without the little mutt. She'd been the only constant in his life since he arrived in New Brunswick.

His cell vibrated in his pocket, and he pulled it out.

"Hello. Chase? Good to hear from you, man." His voice reflected genuine enthusiasm. In spite of their often competitive stance, he and his brother loved each other and were good friends. "What's new? Everyone okay?" He listened, then let out his best cowboy "Yehaw! A son! Congratulations, brother! Mother and boy doing well? Terrific." Another pause, then, "Yeah, I will be out to see him…soon. You got a name yet? Jordan? After our favorite country singer? Great. When we get together, I have a great yarn to spin…about that name."

As he punched off, he was grinning. "Guess we've just got ourselves one great big legitimate reason to be Alberta bound, buddy," he told Fox.

****

"Hey, birthday girl." Ross stepped into the farmhouse kitchen littered with discarded bright gift wrappings, the table in the center bearing the recent carnage of cake and ice cream.

"Oh, Uncle Ross!" Katie Rose struggled out from a mound of toys and brightly colored paper to rush to him, face flushed. "You missed the best party ever!"

"I can see that." He grinned at Jake and Shelby, collapsed in chairs. "Sure looks like it was a real whingding."

"What's that? Whingding?" She looked up at him, wide-eyed in a way he'd discovered could melt him like a popsicle in a microwave.

"Good time."

"Whingding." Ross guessed she was adding it to her vocabulary. Glancing over at Shelby, he was relieved to see it got a wry nod of approval.

"Sit." Katie Rose indicated a chair at the table. "You have to have some cake."

"Sure, okay, but why don't you cut me a piece while I go out to my truck? I need to get something."

"Okay." She climbed onto a chair and reached for the knife resting beside the remains of the cake.

"Let me help." Shelby came to her side and modified the size of the serving from a third of what was left of the cake to a more reasonable helping.

Grinning, Ross went out to his truck. Shortly he was back, carrying a pony saddle, matching bridle, and a three-foot-high stuffed pink rabbit. Katie Rose's eyes widened as he'd never seen before as she sucked in a deep breath.

"Oh, Uncle Ross!" Her face lit up in a huge smile.

"Oh, Ross!" Shelby shook her head ruefully, but she, too, was smiling.

"Just a few things I picked up today in town." He found himself suddenly feeling shy under the happy attention he was attracting.

"I'm sure." Shelby came to stand beside her daughter as the little girl dropped to her knees beside the gifts. "That saddle and bridle were custom made, or I don't know anything about riding equipment."

"I might have talked to a guy about it a while back."

"Yes, you might have."

"Uncle Ross, can we put these on Pretty right

now?" Hugging the rabbit, Katie Rose gazed up at him.

"In the morning, honey." Shelby took her daughter's hand, sticky with cake, and helped her to her feet. "Anyway," she hurried on as a lower lip pouted out, "Pretty's probably asleep. Wash your hands and you can watch the Bugs Bunny video your dad gave you. Then it's off upstairs for a much-needed bath."

"Okay." The word came out slowly, reluctantly. "Want to watch it with me, Uncle Ross?"

"I'd like to, but I have to get back to the farm. Fox will be wanting her supper."

"Why didn't you bring her with you?" she asked.

"She was asleep, and I didn't want to wake her," he lied, not wanting to say he'd been afraid a birthday party with a bunch of sugar-fueled five-year-olds might be too much for the dog.

"Okay." She headed for the parlor, but Shelby caught her up in her arms and carried her to the sink to wash sticky hands.

"Now you can turn on the DVD player," she said, replacing her daughter on the floor.

"Don't forget to eat your cake, Uncle Ross," the child said as she headed into the next room holding the big rabbit and looking back at him. She ran the stuffed toy into the doorframe and promptly sat down unexpectedly on the floor. "He's a big bugger, isn't he? Excuse me, Mommy," she continued as her mother rolled her eyes toward the ceiling. "I meant to say he's a big bunny."

"Of course you did." Shelby crossed her arms and gave her daughter a mildly admonishing look.

Unabashed, Katie Rose scrambled to her feet and gathered up the rabbit.

Grinning, Ross sat down at the table and took the fork Shelby handed him as the little girl scurried into the living room.

"Milk?" Shelby went to the refrigerator.

"Sure." He remembered his objection to milk the first time Jessi had put it in front of him, but over her days with him, he'd developed a taste for it…or maybe a desire not to disappoint her.

"Jake, what are we going to do about Katie Rose's vocabulary? If she keeps on using that kind of language, she'll be expelled on her first day of school." She poured out a glass, then sank down on a chair across from Ross.

"Not to worry. She's learning. Did you see how quick she was to correct herself and apologize, just now? That's progress."

"I guess." Shelby heaved a sigh.

"Good. Hold the thought. Man, am I beat." Jake sat, as well. "Ten five-year-olds full of cake and ice cream can make one amazing amount of noise and confusion."

"Worse than a bunch of half-wild groupies after your body and soul?" Ross slanted him a sly grin.

"Jake…" Shelby looked over at her husband, astonishment in her glance.

"Ross knows. He caught me singing in the barn the other day, and I confessed."

"And were you surprised?" Shelby asked.

"Surprised is putting it way too soft." He finished the cake, downed the milk, and stood. "I never knew a genuine celebrity before."

"You're leaving?" Jake asked as Ross slapped on the Stetson he'd removed before sitting down at the table. "Hang around. Once that cake and milk settles, we can have a beer while Shelby gets one very tired, sticky kid to bed."

"No, thanks. I need to get home and finish closing up the place. I want to get an early start in the morning. Aside from attending the birthday bash, I dropped in to say good-bye. Fox and I are heading home...to Alberta."

"Did you call Jessi?" Shelby's words came out with eagerness.

"No, I got a call from my brother. He and his wife Janet had a baby boy. I need to be introduced to my nephew."

"That's wonderful news!" Shelby gave him a hug, then stepped back to look up into his face. "But you will be seeing Jessi when you get out there?"

"Not sure she'll want to see me."

"Ross Turner, you're not afraid of a two-thousand-pound bull, but one small woman..." Shelby put her hands on her hips.

"Yeah, you got that right."

"When does your flight leave?" Jake got to his feet. "Do you need a drive to the airport?"

"Thanks, but no. Fox and I are driving. I bought my rented truck some time back."

"Driving? Man, it's November. We could get a snowstorm anytime now. And it's thousands of miles." Jake faced him, his expression grave.

"Yeah, well, I don't want Fox shipped in an airline crate clear across this country. Look after this guy, Shelby. He's still not the world's best rider."

"I will."

He gathered her into a bear hug. When he released

her, he held out a hand to Jake. "Till we meet again, my friend. And thanks."

"For what? You're the one who saved our daughter."

"You know for what. Now I have to go. Say good-bye to the kid for me."

"I'll get her." Shelby started for the parlor door.

"No!" Ross stopped her with more vehemence than he'd intended. Then, more softly, "No."

"Understood." Jake nodded and slapped him on a shoulder. "Good luck. We'll be rootin' for you. Let us know how it goes."

"Sure will. Oh, and by the way…" He paused in the doorway. "They named the kid Jordan, after my brother's and my favorite country singer."

Chapter Twenty

The windshield wipers couldn't cut it. The Alberta snowstorm was too much for their slashing sweeps. Ross could barely see ten feet in front of the truck. *Jesus, what a night.* Then he stopped himself. Have to stop cussing.

In the passenger bucket seat, Fox lay curled up in a blanket, eyes wide open. She hadn't slept since they'd driven into the storm just over the Alberta border. She seemed to sense they were in trouble as Ross struggled to keep the truck on what he assumed was the road in the whiteout.

We should have pulled off at that last town. Ross's gloved hands gripped the wheel with a vengeance. *But, damn it, five more hours and we can be home...well, maybe six or seven, in these rotten conditions.*

The truck swerved, swirled, and catapulted off the road.

Ross's head flew forward and hit the steering wheel as his vehicle jammed to a stop, nose buried in a snowbank.

****

"Sir, are you okay? Can you open the door?"

Ross came back to a blurry consciousness, aware of someone banging against the window on his left side and Fox's indignant barking.

What happened? He struggled to clear his head as

he turned slowly toward the noise to see eyes peering in at him through a framework of snow.

"Yeah, yeah." He swallowed hard, rubbed his forehead, and lowered the window.

The blast of cold air helped to clear away some of the cobwebs of confusion and pain. "What happened?"

"You spun off the road." The man he was now recognizing as a mountie informed him. "I've called for a tow truck. It should be here any minute. Sure you're okay? How about the little dog?"

Ross turned to Fox, who'd stopped barking. "Okay, girl?"

She wagged her tail.

"Yeah, she's fine."

"Would you mind stepping out, sir?" The officer moved back to allow Ross to force his way out through the snow piled against the driver's door.

"I haven't been drinking, Officer." Ross shoved his way out of the vehicle and faced the mountie.

"Have to check," he replied. "Although I know anyone could spin out of control on these roads. There's a motel with a restaurant and gas bar about five miles up ahead. I think you should check in there once you're back on the road. Fatigue can be almost as bad as drinking. Nothing can be so important as to risk your life on roads like this."

"I'm heading home to see my nephew. He was born last Friday."

"Congratulations. Is the child well? And his mother?"

"Both hale and hearty as far as I know."

"Then there's no rush. I'm sure the boy will still be there if you arrive a few hours later than you'd planned."

"You're right, Officer. Kid's not going anywhere."

An hour later, as Ross settled for sleep in the bed of a seedy motel, he grimaced as he touched his forehead. *Bloody hell, all I've got is a big headache, nothing near serious enough to bring Jessi rushing to my side. Damn it, what gave me that thought? Jake and Shelby analogy? I'm going home to see my nephew. Must have banged my head harder than I thought.*

****

"He is one good-looking guy." Ross grinned down at his nephew in his arms. He'd found Janet and Chase at his parents' house when he arrived at the Turner ranch. "Looks a lot like his mother, lucky kid." He winked over at Janet.

Jordan Turner screwed up his small face and wailed.

"Time for lunch." Janet took her son back into her arms and headed upstairs.

"Where did he get that outfit?" Ross turned to his mother after they'd gone. " 'Cowboy' on the back of sleepers that small?"

"Jessi brought it over yesterday." Laura Turner turned casually back to checking the roast in the oven. "I think she had it specially made. He is fourth-generation cowboy, after all."

"Jess was here? Yesterday?" Forgetting to play it cool and disinterested, Ross asked quicker than he knew he should have.

"Actually, she's been here a few times since Jordan was born." His mother shoved the roaster back inside and closed the oven door. "She's really fond of the little fellow. She'll make a great mother. Hopefully she'll meet a good man who will make that possible some day." Humming she went to the sink and began peeling potatoes.

"Someday?" Ross followed her. "Someday? I thought you had Jess and me all but married. I thought…"

"So did I, dear." Laura half turned to him and smiled. "But I was wrong. I see now that you and Jessi weren't meant to be a couple. She's devoted to her home and work, while you'll no doubt be going back on the circuit. Furthermore, after her experience with Clint Harrison, I don't think she'll ever want to get serious about a rodeo cowboy again. I obviously misread the entire situation." She paused and looked musingly off into space.

"Now, there's that nice young man from down Smokey Lake way. Joan tells me he's been up here more than once, looking for horses. I understand he's more or less taken over his father's place these past few years." She went back to peeling potatoes. "Actually, I was thinking Wrangler might be just what he's looking for."

"Wrangler? Wrangler?" His horse's name burst from Ross twice in his agitation. "I hardly think so. Wrangler isn't for sale. Not to some guy from Smokey Lake that I've never clapped eyes on. And you can tell Jess for me I don't appreciate her suggesting…"

"Jessi didn't suggest any such thing." His mother glanced sideways at him. "I imagine she knows you too well to believe you'd be willing to give up Wrangler at any price. I simply thought it might be good for the horse to be somewhere he can do the work he was bred to do, the work he enjoys. The same goes for Jessi, in a way." She peeled a length of skin from a potato, her attention apparently on her work. "She needs a place to settle down and do what she does best."

"Your mother's right." Tall, broad-chested, blue-eyed Bob Turner, from his seat at the kitchen table, joined the conversation. "Fine girl, Jessi Wallace. She deserves nothing but the best."

"Yeah, well." Feeling chafed to the bone, Ross rubbed his palms on the seat of his jeans. "Okay, sure, fine. Just remember, my horse isn't for sale...especially not to some guy from Smokey Lake who's up here putting the moves on Jess. Now, I'm going down to the barn to visit Wrangler until dinner's ready."

He grabbed his jacket from a peg by the door.

"I'll go with you." Chase followed his example.

As they walked down to the barn, Chase swung an arm about his brother's shoulders.

"Damn it, Ross." He chuckled. "I thought you were smarter than that."

"What do you mean?" Ross stopped short and scowled at his brother.

"Mom's playing you. Dad, too. Reverse psychology."

"You mean...?"

"Yes, I mean. Mom is still dead set on getting you and Jessi paired up...Dad, too. They know you pretty darned well. If throwing you together didn't work, then making it seem exactly the wrong thing to do might just be the answer. Sure, there was a guy up here from Smokey Lake, but he wasn't putting the moves on Jess. He was just looking for good stock. And Mom and Dad would never sell Wrangler...well, that is, unless you'd acted like anything other than a gentleman when you and Jess were sharing that old farmhouse in New Brunswick. And even then…"

"So you're saying…"

"Yeah, I'm saying they're still as hot as ever to get you married off to her."

They continued on to the barn. Once inside, Ross went to the box stall where his gelding Wrangler stood, head thrust out to greet him. The horse whinnied a greeting.

"Good to see you, too, boy," Ross rubbed his snout. "I'll take you for a run tomorrow, promise."

"He's been restless, Ross." Chase moved on to another stall with steel bars. "Maybe you *should* consider selling him. Not much sense in you keeping him when you're never home. Now this guy"—he put his hand in to pat the stallion inside—"has been living up to his name as a gentleman since Jessi worked with him. I've been riding the Grey Gent a fair amount since she got him settled. I sure as hell wouldn't do that if I thought there was a serious chance of getting pelted. I have a family to think of these days."

"Don't you start trying to manipulate me, too." Ross rubbed the horse under his forelock. "Wrangler will be getting lots of exercise. I'm planning to stick around…for a while. But don't say anything to Mom. She'll be planning flower arrangements and surfing the Internet for dresses the minute you do."

"Ross, what was it caused the rift between you two back in New Brunswick? Had to be something pretty serious. Jessi came home, unexpected as roses in January. She never explained it to anyone, that I know of. Not something really stupid…the old wine, women, and song bit?"

"It was whisky, and only one woman, and I sure as hell wasn't singing." Ross kept focused on his horse. "Cat Holt and Clint Harrison showed up."

"Oh."

"Yeah. Oh. Jess and I had this stupid fight, and we both went off separately with them…first Cat and I to her hotel room—where I assure you nothing happened aside from her throwing a glass of whisky in my face—and then Jess and Clint to a fancy dinner at an expensive restaurant. Then…" He stopped. God, it all sounded so high school.

"Then?" His brother leaned against the stall beside him and crossed his arms. Ross could tell he wasn't going anywhere until he got the whole story.

"Then Clint made a pass at Jess, started getting nasty, and I stepped in, he took a swing at me…long story short, we had one whale of a fight and both of us ended up in jail. Before I could explain, Jess hightailed it for Alberta without knowing that nothing happened between me and Cat…that nothing will ever happen between that woman and me."

"Hell, is that all?" Chase turned away to pick up a hay fork.

"Is that all?" Ross stopped him before he could enter a stall. "Isn't it enough? Jessi isn't into one-night stands, and much as she understands the lifestyle of some rodeo cowboys, she isn't about to fall for any guy who is part of it…like she discovered Harrison is. Only you wouldn't understand, you who went off to university, who never got into any scrapes."

"Listen, little brother." Clay put a hand on Ross's shoulder. "Don't nominate me for sainthood so fast. I had my times at college…my share of wine, women, and song. I think most men have to get a certain amount of craziness out of their systems before they're ready to settle down."

"You…wine, women, and song? Hell and high water, Chase. I always thought…Mom and Dad always believed…"

"Maybe Mom, but definitely not Dad. He actually gave me a lecture on safe sex the day before I left for university."

"Dad? Why didn't I come in for this talk? Why…?"

"Because you took off before he had a chance. Later, I guess he assumed you'd learned on your own." He continued into the stall. "So go see Jessi. Explain everything to her. She's got a lot of common sense. I'm pretty damned sure she'll accept a cowboy's confession…just like Janet did."

****

A hazy winter sun peeked over the trees late the following afternoon as Ross led a saddled Wrangler out of the barn. He'd lunged him in the round pen and realized his parents and brother had been right. The horse was in desperate need of exercise. He would have taken him out first thing in the morning but it had seemed more important to help Chase with ranch chores, to give him more time with his wife and child. Now that Ross had his horse reasonably quieted, he planned to go for a long ride up into the frost-trimmed trees above the hayfields. Later, maybe, if he got up the courage, he'd drive over to the Wallace ranch. Maybe.

He was about to swing into the saddle when he saw a maroon king cab, with a horse trailer attached, driving into the yard. It drove past the house, out to where Ross stood, stopped, and Jack Wallace swung out.

"'Afternoon, Ross." He came forward to greet his neighbor's son, an affable grin on his ruggedly handsome face, right hand extended. "Heard you were home. Good to see you, boy."

"Good to see you, too, Jack." Ross accepted his greeting. "Getting or bringing?" He indicated the trailer.

"Oh, getting. Your dad called last night and said the Grey Gent needed more work and would Jessi have time to get him straightened out. So…"

Warning bells went off in Ross's head. Hadn't Chase just told him the stallion was behaving well, that he'd been riding him?

"I'm surprised Jessi didn't come for him herself." Ross scratched Wrangler under his forelock, avoiding Jack Wallace's eyes.

"Yeah, well…" The man looked down at his boots and shifted them in the light snow. "She was busy."

"Not comfortable playing cupid, Jack?" Ross broke into a grin. Man, who could resist these people? Furthermore, he didn't want to. Not any more.

"Damn it, Ross, we all know you and my girl would make a great team." He squinted over at Ross. "Your mother and my wife are just determined to give the situation a boot in the backside."

"Yeah, well, boot received. So let's get down to business, Jack. Is this just too outdated or do I still have to get your permission to ask your daughter to marry me?"

"Hell, how would I know, Ross?" He grinned over at the younger man. "But if you're asking, sure, go ahead, with my blessing…or whatever I'm supposed to say." He shook hands with Ross again, nodded, and turned back to the truck and trailer. "I have to go in to Calgary, so I'll leave the trailer here. No need to drag along something that was only a smokescreen anyway. Give me a hand to unhitch."

"Sure." Feeling happier than he had in months, Ross went to assist his hopefully future father-in-law.

"But, Ross." Jack Wallace paused when they'd finished unhitching the trailer. "You might have some work to do first. I'm not sure what happened that last while down in New Brunswick, but Jessi came home, from what I could see, more than a bit riled at you. Never gave details, but…"

"Yeah, yeah, I can't say I blame her." Ross leaned against the trailer. "But I can explain…if she'll just listen."

****

"Ross, don't you look nice!" Ross came downstairs to find his mother taking a golden brown pie from the oven.

"Clean shirt and jeans are hardly fancy." He pulled on the sheepskin-lined rancher's jacket he carried and reached for his Stetson on a peg by the door.

"But a midday shower?" She gave an appreciative sniff.

"Okay, okay." He grinned over at her. "Will it make your day to know you might be on the road to getting what you wanted?"

"And what might that be?" She shot him an innocuous glance.

"I'm heading over to see Jessi."

"Really? Well, drive carefully." She turned back to the stove.

"I will." He stared at her back, puzzled. "Come on, Fox. Jess will be glad to see you, anyway."

He had his hand on the doorknob when his mother lost her battle to remain disinterested. She crossed the kitchen in a rush to hug her tall son. "Good luck, honey," she whispered, a catch in her voice.

"Yeah, well, I'll need it." He swallowed a quiver of emotion, kissed the top of her head, and stepped outside, his little red dog at his heels.

Chapter Twenty-One

Ross drove up to the rail fence in front of the Wallace ranch house and got out. It had started to snow as he left his home. Now it had all the earmarks of one heavy storm. He shoved open the gate and headed toward the verandah.

"Ross!" Joan Wallace burst out the door. "I'm so glad to see you!"

She rushed down the steps and into his arms.

"Good to see you, too, Mrs. Wallace." Although pleased with the woman's greeting, he was more than a bit astonished at its vehemence.

"Jessi went up into the hills, looking for that little palomino she's been working with." Joan Wallace's words spilled out as she looked up at Ross, her face creased with lines of concern. "A customer's truck backfired as he was leaving, and the mare panicked and took off. Jessi rode after her just as the first flakes started to fall. Jack is gone to Calgary on business, and I hate to leave this place alone. Ross, will you…?"

"Which is your best horse…the one that can keep his hooves under him in snow?"

"That would be Badger. He's the buckskin in the first stall on the left."

"Good." He released her and headed for the barn with long, determined strides. "Come on, Fox," he called to the little dog who'd jumped from the truck when he got out.

"Thanks, Ross," Joan called after him.

He waved a dismissive hand without turning back, Fox at his heels. He had to find Jessi. Maybe the little dog could once again work her magic.

****

White. Everything around him appeared to be an endless blanket of white. Snow slanted into his eyes. He pulled his Stetson lower as he squinted into the swirling flakes.

"Jess!" he bellowed for what must have been the hundredth time, at least. "Jess!"

Beneath him, Badger shook his head. His mane had frozen, frost had made a rim around his snout, but he hadn't once faltered.

Poor old devil must find it damned uncomfortable, but he's one great horse. Joan gave me the right one. He's tough as nails and not about to give in to a bit of weather.

Plugging ahead, Ross turned the collar of his sheepskin-lined jacket higher.

Damn, it's cold. Gloves aren't doing their job. My fingers are getting numb. Jess, where in hell are you?

****

A winter twilight was beginning to descend and Ross had all but given up hope of finding her before complete darkness engulfed him when Fox, who'd been running ahead, paused and sniffed the air like a pointer. Badger turned his head to the right and whinnied. A horse answered.

"Where, Fox? Show me." Ross swung in the saddle, looking in the same direction as the horse. "Go, girl. Find Jessi."

The dog gave a sharp bark and headed toward a grove of naked birches about fifty yards away. In the deepening darkness and driving snow, Ross recognized the silhouette of a horse. A horse with reins hanging to the ground. Something jumped in his chest.

He turned and sent the old horse plunging through the rapidly accumulating snow.

Once beside the animal, he jumped to the ground. Standing a few feet away, head bent over a mound in the snow, rope dangling from its neck, was an animal barely recognizable as a palomino, so encrusted was it from the elements. Fox set up an insistent barking over the immobile lump.

"Jess!" He floundered to join the dog, dropped to his knees, and pulled her out of the drift and into his arms. "Jess!" He shook her roughly, desperately.

You have to be alive, you have to!

She moved and moaned. Her eyes opened slowly.

"Ross." He'd never thought his own name could sound so good, so perfect.

"Yeah, Ross." He fought to make light of the situation. He couldn't handle anything else. "Got yourself into a fine mess this time, lady."

"Big cat startled my horse." The words came out thick, struggling. "I wasn't paying attention…trying to get a rope on Maisy."

"You got throwed." He had to joke…had to or his voice would crack. "Come on…" He gathered her up in his arms and began to struggle through the storm toward Badger. "I brought a bomb-proof fella. He'll get us home, big cats or not."

"Badger?" She turned her head slightly to look at the horse. *Good. She was coming out of it…at least enough to recognize the horse.* "You rode Badger?"

"Your mom's recommendation." He hoisted her into the saddle. When he felt she could remain there, he went to gather up her mount's reins and the rope dangling from the palomino's neck. When he finally vaulted up behind her, with both horses in tow, she slumped against his chest.

"Take me home, Ross." The words were the sweetest mumble he'd ever heard.

"You got it, lady. Come on, Badger, Fox. Home."

****

"How is she?" Ross turned from the darkened ranch house window where he'd been staring out into the blizzard. His jaw worked in a tick he couldn't control as Joan Wallace returned to the warm kitchen with its fire crackling on the stone hearth.

"Sleeping." A weak smile curled her lips. "She'll be fine, Ross, thanks to you."

"Don't forget Fox and Badger." He was able to grin in return.

"Of course." She looked fondly down at the dog curled up on a mat near the fire. "I think I might just have a very large beef bone for you, Fox."

She went to the refrigerator and took out a treat that made Fox's head come up and her ears perk. When Joan laid it in front of her, the little dog heaved a sigh of pleasure before attacking the meal.

"Can I see her?" Ross couldn't stop himself asking.

"I think you'd best wait for morning." Joan Wallace touched his arm gently. "She's exhausted."

"Sure." He sank into a chair at the table. His boots sat drying by the fire, his coat hung thawing around the back of a chair beside them, and he felt a weariness enveloping him. "I'll just sit here for a bit and rest up."

"Fine." Joan Wallace put another log on the fire and replaced the screen in front of it. "I assume you've called your family to let them know you're safe? Good. I'll be off to bed, then. There are cold cuts and beer in the refrigerator and bread in the box on the counter. If you feel you need something stronger, help yourself to Jack's bar in his office."

"Beer and a sandwich of cold cuts sound just fine, thanks, Joan. I've sworn off the hard stuff."

"Well, good for you. The guest room is on the right at the top of the stairs. I'm sure you're ready for rest. And, Ross"—she paused on her way out of the kitchen—"a hundred thousand thank-yous."

****

"Ross?" His name spoken softly jolted him out of his sleep. In front of him, an opened bottle of beer with little more than a mouthful missing sat on the table beside an uneaten sandwich. Standing in the kitchen was a vision in a pair of flannelette pajamas with galloping horses all over them, golden-brown hair falling over her shoulders.

"Jess?" He pulled himself upright and cleared his throat when her name sounded like a croak. "Jess."

"Yes." Smiling, she crossed the room. "Ross, Mom told me what you did. Thank you."

"No need. It was mostly Fox and Badger." He reached for his beer and took a long drink from the bottle, its carbonation long gone. *God, how long have I been asleep?*

Glancing toward the window, he saw early morning sunlight flooding into the room. The room was still warm, but the fire on the hearth had died to a few embers.

"Looks like the beginnings of one very fine day." He pulled himself upright and flinched as cramped muscles came into play. "Guess I never made it to that bed your mother offered."

"Guess you didn't." She headed to the percolator and began to make coffee. "Ross, what brought you back to Alberta?" She spoke with her back to him.

"New nephew."

"Oh, yes, right." She finished setting up the machine but didn't turn back. Instead she stood looking out a window.

"Pretty awesome little guy." Ross struggled to find comfortable conversation.

"Certainly is."

"Wouldn't mind having one of my own someday." He took a giant leap.

"Really?" She swung back to face him. "I thought, after Katie Rose got lost, you said…"

"Yeah, well, I was kind of freaked out. I've had time to think since then…and I've met my nephew, and…"

"And?" She crossed the room and startled him by sliding onto his lap.

"And since I've found a lady I think would make a great mother…"

"And might you be in love with this lady who will be the mother of your progeny?"

"Pretty damned…darned sure. And that's an all-out confession. She's made me give up whisky and work on cutting down on the cussing."

"And other women?"

"Jess, about Cat…"

"No need to confess to anything right now. After I had time to think things over, I decided a man who'd get into a fight with that useless bit of trash called Clint Harrison, in order to defend my honor, couldn't be too serious about that bold…witch." She grinned for a moment before looking deep into his eyes and moving forward to put her lips to his. "See, no more unacceptable language from me, either."

Ross's arms went about her, and a complete happiness he'd never felt before enveloped him. No bull riding championship could be as good as this. Him and Jess.

"Ironic, isn't it?" she murmured against his cheek as he pulled her close.

"What?"

"I went to New Brunswick to save you, and you came back to Alberta in time to rescue me."

"Yeah, I guess." But he was only half listening as he bundled her closer into his arms, as thoughts of kissing her and so much more distracted him.

"Well, well." They broke apart but Jessi remained on his knee as Jack Wallace came into the kitchen, stamping snow from his boots. "Caught you, young fella. Now you have no choice but to marry my daughter and make an honest woman of her."

"Guess so." Ross grinned at Jessi. "Find a parson, and we'll get right to it."

"Ah, now, that won't work at all, at all." Jack Wallace shed his Stetson and coat and headed across the kitchen to put a big hand on the coffeepot. "Damn! Cold."

"I must have forgotten to plug it in. It's all set up." Jessi started to rise, but her father waved her back.

"Stay where you are." He shoved the plug into an outlet. "Now, as I was saying," he continued, turning back to the couple. "No quick wedding plans will do. Can you just imagine the stir your mother would kick up, Ross, if she didn't have time to see it done up the way ladies consider right? And that probably would be mild, considering what I'd have to face here. We only have one child, and I'm damned sure Joan isn't about to let her get married in anything less than stellar style."

"Okay, fine." Ross emitted a half-groan. "Then, when?" He looked at Jessi.

"I'm thinking Valentine's Day."

"Hell...heck, that's not until February!"

"Yes, but we do want Shelby and Jake and Katie Rose and maybe even Grady, if he'll agree, to be able to come." She grinned at him. "And we can't ask them to leave their family over Christmas. They told me they have a big party planned at the farm. So Valentine's is the next holiday...and the most romantic."

"Ah, now, baby girl." Her father used his pet name for her as he leaned back against the counter to wait for the coffee to brew. "That's a long time to ask any fella to wait."

"It's okay, Jack." Ross was grinning. "I spent a lot of time already with this lady driving me crazy. I'm pretty damned...darned sure I can wait a bit longer."

"What's all this stumbling over the cuss words?" Jessi looked at him.

"Not good language to use around kids. I'm trying to cut back, just in case..."

He didn't finish. Jessi's lips had stopped his words.

Discover the romance between Shelby and Jake in *Counterfeit Cowboy* and learn more about Officer Frasier MacKenzie, Emma, and their amazing Pug in *Holding off for a Hero*, also by Gail MacMillan and available from The Wild Rose Press.

A word about the author...

Award-winning author of 35 published books, Gail is a graduate of Queen's University and a four-time winner of Maxwell Medals for her dog books. Heather, the heroine of her historical romance *Heather for a Highlander*, was recently named the best heroine of 2014 by the Canadian Romance Writers, winning their Maple Leaf Award.

Visit Gail at:

macgail@nbnet.nb.ca